MW01531646

Missing Key

Scott Musial

Copyright © 2010 Scott Musial

All rights reserved.

ISBN: 978-0-9848783-1-4

For you Babe.

Thank You

To my children, Alexandria and Christopher. Your strengths at such a young age, are an encouragement to me. You both help to drive me to do more in my life.

To my mother and father. Whatever you did to me while I was growing up, thank you.

To Kelley. You are the reason for this book. Without you I never would have started it, stuck with it, or finished it.

Chapter 1

Jennifer Kelley was driving west along State Road 24 on her way to the quiet little seaside town of Cedar Key. She had never been to this little island before, and she wondered to herself why she had agreed to go there now. Having left Jacksonville a few hours earlier she had passed through the central counties of northern Florida without too much excitement. Now with only twenty minutes until her destination, she was looking forward to getting out of her confining trap of a rental car and enjoying a stiff martini.

As the wispy needles that clung tightly to the swaying branches of the Cypress and Pine trees, and the sharp fat leaves of the Palmetto bushes opened themselves to the vast views of the Gulf waters, Jennifer could feel an excitement start to build inside her. With all the strong rotting fish smells of the creeks and marsh lands, and the gorgeous landscape views of the sun and sky as they danced together across the living waves, she immediately lost any doubt that she originally had about making this trip. She had always loved being close to salt water and as she drove along the short causeway that connected the little islands leading out to Cedar Key she immediately felt at home. Right then, more than ever before, she really wanted that drink.

As she passed into Cedar Key, Jennifer continued straight on State Road 24 before turning left onto Second Street. After traveling two blocks to the East she parked in the street directly in front of the Island Hotel and Restaurant.

The hotel was one of the oldest buildings on the island, and its only Bed and Breakfast. A roof covered second floor balcony, stretched the two lengths of the building and shadowed the sidewalks along Second and B Streets. From the balcony hung flags of The United States, Britain and Florida as well as some of the states favorite colleges. These flags all hung from their stanchions rippling gently in the light breeze that was blowing in from the sea.

Jennifer crossed the paved narrow street onto the sidewalk that was under the balcony and up the stairs that lead to the double doored main entrance. She reached for one of the old metal door knobs that looked to be an original fixture here, and turning it carefully she had to give the door a little shove to unstick it from its lifelong mate. The hinges hesitated, reluctant to open at first, and then let out a long guttural squeak as if they were saying to her, "Please be gentle with me, I'm in my declining years." Crossing the threshold and into the large welcoming lobby she immediately noticed a large stuffed manatee that sat at a baby grand piano to her right. Further examination of the room also revealed some rather large leather chairs and a sofa that seemed to invite customers and staff together for an evening of gossip and good old fashioned conversation.

Straight ahead of her sat an abandoned counter that ran along the left wall of the room, and appeared to be the main desk. As she approached, she rang the small stainless steel desk bell on the counter to alert someone to her arrival. While she was waiting for some assistance she scanned through the guest registry and read through some of the comments of previous visitors to the hotel. '*We had a great time, Can't wait to come back and visit again. Stayed the weekend in room 36 and dreamed of the movie stars that had stayed in there before us. An absolute must visit.*' Adding a quick note of her own, Jennifer simply stated, '*this is my first visit to this island and I am already enchanted by all that I have seen.*' She realized that she hadn't seen very much at all yet, but she had seen enough to be intrigued and didn't want to forget to make a comment in the book later. She just looked at it as being proactive.

As she finished writing her comments in the book, she saw a woman come in from the doorway to the left, that attached the lobby to the hotel's restaurant. In a lovely deep British accent she said to

Jennifer, "Sorry to keep you waiting my dear, I've been bussing a few tables. How may I help you?"

"I have a reservation." Jennifer said.

"Very well." The woman responded, and after looking through a short stack of index cards that she had retrieved from a coverless shoebox, she looked up and stated, "You must be Jennifer."

"Why yes I am. That's a very good trick." Jennifer said with an amazed look on her face.

The woman gave her a broad gentle smile, and holding the index card up for Jennifer to see, said to her, "You're my only reservation for tonight dear."

Jennifer gave her own broad smile back at the woman.

"Come with me." The woman insisted, "I will take you upstairs and give you the grand tour."

Jennifer followed the woman up the stairs where they turned immediately to the right into a dimly lit hallway that had several doors. Each of these doors sheltered its own private and unique little room.

"All of these rooms down here share this central bathroom." The woman told her as she pointed to the small room on her right. "The rooms are all very comfortable and if you are looking to see one of our ghosts during your stay, you stand the best chance down on this end."

"Ghosts?" Jennifer asked, not sure if she was shocked by this statement or just genuinely curious.

"Oh yes," she smiled, "we have several that wander around. It just seems like most of the sightings by any of our visitors happen in these rooms down here."

"Have you ever seen any of them?"

"Oh yes, my dear." She confirmed. "My favorite is a woman who appeared to me downstairs in the lobby one afternoon. She was dressed in a light blue dinner gown that appeared to be from the civil war era as well as a broach around her neck that must have weighed an American pound. She just stood there and looked directly at me with an inquisitive expression on her face until finally I asked her if I could help her."

"Did she respond to you?"

"Yes, I believe she did. She vanished."

Jennifer thought about this for a moment as they headed back to where they had come up the stairs to the second floor. Passing the stairs now they entered into a large open sitting room that had several books and games for the guests to read and play during their stay. The walls of this room were all white painted wood slats that were hung horizontal around the room and extended into two other hallways that led off to other guest rooms. Halfway up this wall and continuing around the entire space was a mural that depicted the landscape and natural beauty of the gulf waters and seashore of the area. The hallway that continued straight ahead had doors to the left and right that closed off more guest rooms and then at the very end was the door that lead out to the wrap around balcony that she had seen from the street.

"These rooms here, each have their own private bathrooms inside." The woman continued, "We have movie stars and musicians that have visited us over the years and they always stay in the rooms out here."

They looked inside each of the rooms one at a time and then once they had seen them all, the woman stated, "You may pick whichever room you like."

"No one else is here?" Jennifer asked.

"Not today my dear. The weekend will be packed though. Good choice to come in on a Thursday."

Thinking back to the comment that she had read in the book downstairs at the front desk, Jennifer looked at the woman and said, "I think that I will take room thirty-six."

Jennifer retrieved her clothes from her rental car and unpacked them into the drawers of the antique dresser. This was a habit that she had started years ago when she traveled as a photojournalist. She had always hated living out of a suitcase and found that unpacking her things immediately when she had arrived anywhere made her feel a lot more comfortable during her stay.

After she had settled into her room, she turned on the water in the tiny shower stall and stripped out of her shorts and T-shirt. Stepping into the hot cascade, she let it pour down onto the top of her head and shoulders and closed her eyes as she felt the steady streams run down her neck and over her breasts and stomach before accelerating down her legs and pooling beneath her feet.   The steaming hot water rejuvenated her as it washed away the dirt and sweat from her day of traveling and it prepared her for a relaxing night of drinking.

After she had fully unwound with the long shower, she put on a small black dress that revealed a little too much cleavage and a very generous amount of her thigh.   This was her favorite dress for an evening on the town because she knew the effect that it had on anyone that saw her in it. She wore it specifically for those glaring and admiring glances that came from both men and women alike. Without bothering to dry her hair, Jennifer started out of her room and down the stairs that lead to the hotel lobby. The little island had already made some adjustments to her attitude and inner clock. She could feel herself slowing down to the rhythms of island time.

Chapter 2

Downstairs at the hotel bar the night's drinking was just getting started.   The Neptune's Lounge was a very small bar that sat in the back corner of the hotels first floor and its presence was made known by a small sign above the door that simply stated, '*Ale - BAR - Beer.*' Underneath that sign sat another one that simply pointed into the room with an arrow and had one word printed on it, '*Restrooms.*' Once you made your way inside this tiny space you immediately looked directly into the eyes of the bar's namesake.   A large painting of Neptune, with his trident in hand, hung high on the wall behind the bar so that he could watch over his devoted servants as they enjoyed their libations.   Two bullet holes that marred this painting, without so much as a scratch on the god of the sea, told the story of another nights festivities in here and the half crazed antics that must have followed.   The walls surrounding the room were painted with a mural much like the wide open walls of the gathering room at the top of the stairs.   This mural scene however was that of fishing boats and docks that reached out from their shoreline perches into the waters of the gulf. It also depicted the cumulonimbus clouds that are so typical for such an island's landscape, as they reached up from the marvelous mural and up to the blue ceiling sky above. Between the bar stools and the high top tables along the wall, the room could seat about twelve patrons in total. Most of these seats were already taken this evening by local customers who sat with their drinks and boisterously told their stories of the days fishing and all the ones that got away. A tall thin man, who looked to be in his early twenties, was telling of the outlandish behavior that he and his friends had taken part in over the past weekend. He loudly informed his intoxicated audience that the McKinley's cat would surely never be the same again.

To the left of the bar was a doorway that lead into a second room. This room had dark stained cypress walls that held old black and white photographs of past visitors and the parties that they had thrown in those bygone days. This room with it's assorted tables and chairs could seat about twenty additional people and had a small wooden railed stage in the back corner that would most definitely be crowded with any more than two musicians on it. This small stage boasted a clientele of singers that had moved on to fill stadiums full of devoted fans and whose current bands couldn't fit in the entire bar let alone on this platform. In this room, a lone man sat at one of the tables drinking a martini and reading a book.

Jennifer walked up to the bar, which seemed to stop everyones conversations, as they stared in amazement at their new found friend. It must have been years since any of them had seen a little black dress, and she was very sure that they had never seen one worn quite the same way that she did.

Looking at the bartender she calmly said. "Dirty martini please. Belvedere with three stuffed olives."

"Right away," responded the bartender.

The man in the back room looked up from his book when he heard Jennifer's order. He looked up at her for a few moments admiring the little black dress that she was barely wearing. As she got her drink and turned around to find a table, the man had already looked back down into his book.

Jennifer sat at one of the high tops with her martini and took notice to the others at the bar stealing glances of her. Was she really that much of a sight to the people around here? As she sipped her martini she let her mind wonder to all the things that had taken place in the past forty-eight hours.

Just two days ago she had been sitting at the Coq d' Or in Chicago, when a man had approached her about a job that he wanted her to do for him in Florida. He explained that he needed a professional photographer to go and take pictures of all the landscapes, buildings, boats and people of a small gulf coast island. He was looking to make some investments in the area and needed to see everything from a non partisan eye. He would make the trip himself if he had the time, but it would be impossible for him to get away from the city any time soon. At first Jennifer was skeptical about taking such a job that seemed to be so menial for the owner of her own studio, but after returning to her photography studio and finding that the work there had slowed to a near standstill, she had decided that work was work and there were bills to be paid.

She thought now about her city of Chicago. She thought about all the hustling people all decked out in their suits and dresses. People going about their business with an independence and determination that either drove them to their desired success, or ruined them along the way. She was one of them and had been for years. The high rise buildings and the constant roar of the city traffic permeated into her very soul. She never noticed any of the commotion while she was there in her city. Now though, in this little bar on an island that most people had never heard of, she noticed the silence.

After draining the glass of her hard earned martini and eating the vodka soaked olives, she looked again toward the other room with the stage. She was surprised by the fact that the man who had been in there reading was now gone. She couldn't imagine where he could have gone. How could he have walked past her without her noticing? This bar was just too small for that to happen. Drawn by her curiosity, Jennifer got up and walked over to the doorway to the next room. She took a better look around and saw the various tables and chairs sitting empty and waiting for their next customers. The doors for the restrooms sat ajar so she figured that he was not in them, but now she could see that there was another open doorway that lead under the stairwell that she had come down earlier. Looking down the short hallway under the stairs she could see through to the kitchen. This must have been the way that the man had taken out. Maybe he was an employee of the hotel to just exit out the back like that. She pondered this for a very short time and then decided that it was time to see what kind of night life this little island could conjure up.

It was dark outside now, as Jennifer stepped out of the hotel onto the sidewalk along Second Street. The street lights were all on and the shadows from the trees and power lines danced in the streets from the light evening breeze. Turning, she walked down the small pothole filled street that lead to the music and sounds of people in the boats and buildings out by the water. The moon was nearly full and its reflected light shone down upon the neon lit waterfront as well as the small bay of still water which had been created by this man made dock of restaurants and bars. There were small boats and barges floating silently on those shimmering waters and they watched all the people as they moved around their tiny enclosed cove.

The dock was an extension of A Street to the East and acted as a break wall for the small bay to protect it from the sometimes stormy Gulf waters. It connected to C Street at a ninety degree turn and then bridged the opening to the bay and back to the main part of the island making a complete loop. The dock's one way street was lined with restaurants, bars, shops and even a couple of hotels. Motorcycles and cars alike were parked on both sides of the street as a horse drawn carriage made it's way through the path that was left. Half baked people strolled the dimly lit sidewalks under the neon signs and backlit awnings in search of their next beer and shrimp basket. There was a strong sense of nightlife here and you could feel the energy of the people that scurried about the street. The wind was strong on your face as you walked along the open street, and the waves could be clearly heard slapping against the wooden pilings that supported these buildings. Sweet aromas of the fresh seafood cooking in the restaurant kitchens as well as the putrid odor of the dead sea creatures that floated in the nearby bay filled the air. The steady Gulf breeze took these sounds and smells and mixed them all together into a sensory jumbalaya that stirred the heart and mind. This dock had a lively, although imitation feel of a true Florida theme park to it. It was quite the contrast to the slow pace and muddled silence of the old town and hotel just a few short blocks away.

Jennifer wandered down the street past all the shops that had been closed up for the evening. Looking inside the dark windows she could see the conch shells and shark tooth jewelry that were the staples of any trinket shop in Florida. The T-shirts and flower patterned dresses that lined the stores inner walls, hung there with pride to be seen from every corner of the shop, with the hopes of being bought and worn to one of the neighboring watering holes.

Walking further down the street she came upon a man sitting at a card table with his dog and selling a book that he had written about their adventures while traveling across the United States on his bicycle. Jennifer squatted down and patted the golden retriever on the head as it looked up at her from where it had been sleeping near the man and his bicycle. Glancing then up at the man, as he silently looked back at her, she smiled politely and then continued on her walk.

Noticing several rowdy groups of people going up and down a set of stairs that lead to one of the restaurants, Jennifer decided that this may be a good place to get a drink. She followed the lively crowd up the brightly painted purple wooden stairs, with their matching hand rails, and entered through the doors.

Frog's Landing was very busy inside, with the roar of the patrons and live music being played slightly above the level where anyone could carry on a normal conversation. The interior walls were all done up like the knotted wood siding from some cabin along a quiet creek in the hills of western North Carolina. Driftwood hung down from the high white ceiling like chandeliers, dangling just above the many heads that milled about below them. Several exposed wooden beams supported the weight of that ceiling in order to keep it from dropping to the hard wood floor below.

Jennifer walked into the grand room and took notice to all the intricate detail that went into the design and decorating of this place. Once at the bar, she ordered a Corona and listened to the band on the stage as they belted out a stirring rendition of Mustang Sally. This was definitely a local band, and the crowd called out to each one of them in adoration as they swayed in their chairs to the rhythms being pulled out of their finely tuned instruments. Listening to the music she let herself get trapped inside the beautiful melodies and just sat for what seemed like hours, enjoying the atmosphere as it absorbed her into the night.

"Better bring another Corona," she told the bartender. Then remembering that she hadn't eaten in hours, she added, "And a dozen oysters, too."

"Raw or steamed?" the bartender replied.

"Raw," she said, "and extra horseradish."

The bartender nodded and popping the cap off of her beer he set it on the bar in front of her. He added a lime wedge with a smile and then walked off to put in her order for food.

"Thank you," She said to the bartender as he walked off, and then to herself, "These are going down really easy tonight."

When the oysters arrived Jennifer turned and sat up to the bar and enjoyed them with another cerveza. The slimy little mollusks slid quickly down her throat, taking with them the stinging burn of all the horseradish in the cocktail sauce. She took a deep breath as the stinging sensation rose up through her sinus cavity and then brought those expected tears to her eyes. Waiting patiently for the burn to subside, she then took up another half shell and repeated the process.

After finishing her treat of the oysters and beer, she went out through the sliding glass windows, that made up the back wall of the bar. Out on the deck which extended out over the black ocean water, she looked at the moon high in the dark sky and watched the ripples of the its reflection on the water streaming at her. A young couple sat on barstools to her right talking quietly to themselves. The man was sitting with one leg between two of the rails and his foot hanging out over the open water. His other foot was on the rail of his barstool which raised his knee up between his partners thighs. She sat facing directly at him with a slight lean in her posture that brought her close enough to steal a kiss at any given time. What a wonderful way to spend an evening, Jennifer thought. Love and moonlight, that's the kind of things that a true romance is made of. After taking in some of the fresh salty sea air and letting it permeate her every thought, she wandered back through the sliding glass door and went back into the bar. She paid the bartender and tipped him generously for his service, then made her way back out and down to the street.

Strolling past the buildings to where she could finally see the Gulf again, she looked back towards the moon and its reflection. This time, in the ripples of moonlight, she noticed the silhouette of a boat. It had small lights turned on near the front and rear of its length and then one again up top. Other than those few sparkling little lights, it was very quiet out there on the open black sea.

Jennifer looked for a moment out on the evenings water and then slowly, after taking in the deep dark landscape, turned and walked back to the hotel and up the old stairs to the gathering room at the top. Once at the door of her room she looked ahead to the end of the hallway and was drawn to the other door that lead out to the balcony that protruded over the sidewalk below. She went out and leaned on the rail that looked over Second Street. Letting out a quiet sigh of contentment she quietly said to herself.

"I'm just not ready to sleep yet."

Chapter 3

"How does it look, Juan?" The voice came down from above him.

Juan looked up from the deep holds of the boat towards the black clouds that were rolling in the dark sky above. He had been down in the bowels of the Lucille for over an hour now loading the boxes into every empty corner that he could find. As he looked up from the dark depths, he could feel that the rain had started to fall as it hit his face and eyes which caused him to blink sharply and look away.

"We still have a little more room señor," he yelled up to the red haired gringo who was standing on the deck above him wearing a bright yellow foul weather jacket. "How much is left?"

"There is plenty up here, fill every last hole that you can find down there. I need to take as much as I can, this may be my last trip here."

"I understand, señor. I will pack it as tight as I can."

Billy Mackay turned away from the square opening in the deck that the men were using to carefully pass down the boxes to Juan. He looked out across the bay at the dark horizon with its low clouds rolling along at an ever increasing rate. This is going to be an exciting evening he thought to himself. Feeling the drops of rain on his forehead and exposed hands, he crossed the gangplank from the boat onto the dock and made his way into Juan's tiny office where he poured himself a cup of hot coffee. This was probably going to be his last dry moments for the next few days and he figured that he should take full advantage of it.

As he watched the men working in the rain from the window of the office he sipped on the bitter black coffee and thought about his wife back at home in the states. She should be nearly about to burst by now he thought to himself. He remembered the promise that he had made to her as he left nearly a month before. He had guaranteed that he would make it back in plenty of time for the birth of their first child and he fully intended to keep that promise. After making two extra port calls to ensure enough cargo, and the storm that was now brewing out over the gulf, he was beginning to doubt his own words. Surely she would understand when he was there for those first few months of their parenthood. When he was there to help out with all the new responsibilities that would arrive with this baby. Yes, he attempted to convince himself, she will understand if I am a little late.

Billy's thoughts dissipated as he saw Juan climb out of the hold up onto the deck. One of the other men working there grabbed a jacket that was being kept dry under a large tarp and wrapped it over Juan's shoulders. The rain had really started to come down now and the horizon that was recently visible out past the boat had now turned into just a grey blur.

Juan stomped his feet to get some of the water off of them as he entered the office. Billy did not look or even change his expression as he continued to watch the men on board his boat seal everything up for him and get her sea worthy.

Juan took his jacket and hung it on a large nail that extended out from the wood trim work around the large bay window of the office.

"Señor," he said to Billy. "I do not think that you should head out in this storm."

Billy just watched the men work.

"They are saying that this could be a hurricane by tomorrow evening."

Billy finally turned from the window as he saw the last of the men leave his boat and run for the shelter of the large warehouse on the dock.

"I know Juan. I have been listening to the radio here. I have to go though, the federalies are sure to track me here very soon. They are most likely counting on the storm to keep me here." He then gave a little smile. "I may already be a father too, my friend. I need to get home to my wife, she will be needing me."

"Si, Mister Billy. I believe that is true. She will most likely want you alive as well though."

"Yes, Juan, that is also true, but I must still go."

"Si, Mister Billy."

"Will you help me cast off please?"

"Yes, señor. Your boat is all set to go."

Billy buttoned up his jacket and walked out into the pouring rain. Juan quickly grabbed his jacket from the nail and followed him through the door. Out on the dock the two men shook hands and Billy went aboard the Lucille and pulled up the gangplank securing it to the cleats on the side of the boats superstructure with a nylon rope. He then made his way around the open deck checking that everything else was secure and wouldn't slide off into the sea or become airborne in the heavy seas and cause some real damage. Once satisfied, he went inside the pilot house and motioned to Juan to untie the mooring lines that held him to the dock so that he could begin his journey into the dark looming storm over the Gulf.

He had left the engines running while the men were loading the cargo just in case the federalies had shown up and he needed to make a quick departure. This made for a very quick departure now and a quick glance at each of the gauges told him that the Lucille was ready to get underway. Easing the boat into gear he slowly brought the speed up on the diesel engines as he turned the ship's wheel and pointed the nose towards the opening in the break wall and the open waters of the Gulf of Mexico beyond that. Even in the darkness of the night and with the rain falling all around, he could see the crisp white breaks of the black waves out in the gulf. He did not fear nor dread the coming ride that he was heading for. He was a sailor, and had been for his entire life. With well over a hundred terrible storms under his sea legs, he was well prepared and knew exactly what needed to be done. No, he did not fear the weather, but he wasn't exactly looking forward to it either.

Chapter 4

"Hello," a voice said from the dark. "Would you care for a beer?"

Startled, Jennifer quickly looked over her shoulder to the right and noticed that she was not alone. There was a man sitting in the bench swing that was hanging down from the ceiling in the corner of the balcony. She looked through the darkness for a moment towards the man and tried in vain to figure out what to do. Finally she leaned back against the balcony railing and looked at him to study his face. She had a feeling that she recognized him from somewhere, and after a moment, she realized that this was the man that had been sitting in the bar earlier that evening. This was the man with the martini in the other room that was quietly reading his book and then suddenly disappeared.

Breaking the uncomfortable silence that he felt after not receiving an answer to his question the man added, "I like that little black dress you're wearing."

Snapping out of her stare, with a little embarrassment, she finally answered him. "Thank you, it's my favorite dress, and yes, I would love a beer."

Knowing that she shouldn't really be alone in the middle of the night talking to this man that she had never met, she walked over in front of the swing where he was sitting and took a Corona.

"My name is Michael," he said to her.

He sat in the big swing looking at Jennifer. One bare foot stretched out along the thick overstuffed cushions and the other one on the table in front of him, gently pushing the swing back and forth.

Michael had a lean muscular body that she could see in the light of the moon that was reflecting down onto him. Not a bulky muscle bound shape, like he worked out at the gym on a very routine basis, but more like the lean muscular build of an avid runner or a swimmer. His tousled brown hair and unshaven face gave him the look of a seasoned local here or possibly that of a vacationing wino. His blue eyes seemed very focused on her at the moment, but she could see the years and miles in them. Michael did not by any means look old, but his eyes showed great knowledge beyond his years.

On the table near Michael's bare foot was a copy of Herman Wouk's book, *Don't Stop the Carnival.* This must have been the book he was reading in the bar when she first saw him earlier, she thought.

"I'm Jennifer," she finally said to him. "I saw you in the bar earlier. You were with Mister Paperman."

Michael looked down at the book on the table and then smiled up at her.

"Some friends," he said, "I take them with me everywhere. It's very nice to meet you Jennifer. What brings you to Cedar Key?"

"Work."

"Work? What kind of job brings someone here? Fishermen or oyster farmers usually have work here but you don't look too much like either one of those."

"I'm a photographer," she said to him. "I'm down here taking pictures of the area."

"Really? How's that going?" Michael asked.

"I haven't started yet. I just got here a few hours ago. Tomorrow is the big day," she smiled, "I plan to make tracks all over this little island."

Michael laughed, "That shouldn't take you very long. What's your plan for the afternoon?"

She laughed back at him and without answering his question she asked, "Why are you here, Michael?"

"Drinking some beers and visiting some old friends," he said. "More of a vacation for me. Why don't you have a seat?" He sat up and moved over to make room for her on the swing. Jennifer smiled and walked over taking a seat next to him.

"Don't mind if I do." She said with a coy little smile as she sat down next to Michael on the inviting green cushions. Leaning back she lifted her right foot out of her sandal and brought it up underneath her. She then extended her left foot out to rest on the edge of the table in front of them.

Raising up her beer to him in a toast, she said. "Here's to Cedar Key. A quiet little community that loves a stiff drink."

Michael raised up his bottle to hers and tapped the necks together.

"That is Cedar Key all right," he responded. After taking a drink of his beer, he turned to her and asked, "Where are you from Jennifer?"

"Chicago."

"I have a friend from there but have never been myself. Do you like it?"

"It's a great city." She said. "I love it there."

"Seems a little large to me. Too many people and way too many cars."

"It can be. You just need to know where to go and the best ways to get around."

"I guess," he said. "How do you get around?"

"I walk mostly. I live just a few blocks from my work and I hang out in bars and restaurants that are in my neighborhood."

"Yeah? Where do you like to go the most?"

"My favorite place to have a drink is at the Coq d' Or. It's an old bar beneath the Drake Hotel that is rumored to have entertained some of Al Capone's top men back in the day. They had offices in the same building and would hang out in the bar to socialize. You can just feel the presence of these gangsters meeting together and talking about who they were going to kill that day, while you sit at the bar and enjoy a drink. Not to mention the fact that Basil, the bartender there, can make one killer of a dirty martini."

Michael laughed. "I love a good martini. What else do you do there?"

"Well, I love to go for a run along the lakefront. With the wide open views of Lake Michigan off to one side and the towering skyscrapers rising up on the other, it's breathtaking to see while running a few miles to wake up each morning."

Jennifer went on for well over an hour talking about the places that she loved to go to in Chicago. She told him about Navy Pier and the giant Ferris Wheel that she would ride and look out over the whole city. The Aquarium out by the lake and the Museums that she could go to and get lost in for hours, while contemplating the ancient relics and great works of art from some of the world's best known artists. She loved to go to these places and watch the people as they came in and became hypnotized by everything that they would see beyond the timeless doors. She talked about the street vendors and the savory little treats that she loved to eat, even though she knew how bad they were for her. Then there were the fine restaurants in town, where she could go and be treated like royalty by some of the worlds best and most renowned chefs.

Michael listened intently as she told him about all of her favorite things in Chicago. He loved her enthusiasm and the way that her eyes lit up as she told him all that she could about her city. She made it sound so wonderful to him. He decided that evening that he must go there and see it for himself one day.

After a few beers and having told Michael all that she could about Chicago, Jennifer stopped talking and just looked at him for a moment. He was a beautiful man and she found herself attracted to him as she looked into his deep blue eyes. She knew in her mind that the evening must end, and even though she could have stayed up all night talking to him, she reluctantly told him that she had to go.

"Good night Michael," she said. "I really must get some rest tonight. I have a lot to do tomorrow."

"Good night," he responded. "I had a great time talking to you. I really want to see Chicago now."

She smiled. "I'm sorry. I went on and on, didn't I?"

"It was wonderful," he said. "What would you say to dinner and a sunset tomorrow night? Cedar Key has one of the greatest sunsets anywhere."

"That would be great. I like sunsets."

"Good." He replied. "It's a date. I'll meet you tomorrow night then, just before sunset, at Coconuts."

"It's a date then.   Goodnight Michael, I had a very nice time talking with you tonight."   Jennifer smiled as she got up from the swing and headed back to her room.

Chapter 5

Even though the lights of Tampico and the Mexican landscape disappeared quickly behind the stern of Billy's boat, he was not making very good headway into the Gulf due to the turbulent seas pushing back against every turn of his propeller. The clouds were so low now that they nearly touched the tops of each wave as they crested and then toppled violently back into the valleys of each cavernous swell. The black night would soon be turning into a miserable grey as day time came upon this little piece of the world. Billy trudged on to the East with his hopes that the cargo would survive the beating that it was taking in the deep holds of this old World War I military rescue boat.

As the night transitioned into day the weather continued to worsen and Billy heard over his radio that the storm had now been upgraded to the category of tropical storm. Tropical Storm **Candy** was taking its toll on him as he watched his mostly useless radar looking for any other ship traffic or other maritime hazards. He was able to keep a good course just to the north of dead east and knew that this would keep him clear of the Yucatan Peninsula and the shallows that were off the Mexican coast.

The day wore on and Tropical Storm *Candy* continued to build its strength as it headed north over the turbulent waters. The winds across the open sea were now exceeding 50 miles per hour and the rain no longer looked like it fell into the ocean, but seemingly blew straight across the top never touching down. The pilot house was quickly becoming a mess with the items that were normally securely tied down, but were now violent projectiles as they desperately tried to find their way to the floor of the vessel.

Billy was now finding it difficult to keep himself upright with the violent twists and turns of the ship's deck caused by the Gulf's waves. They were tearing at the hull trying to take the boat apart board by board and make yet another man made reef at her bottom. Billy was now starting to entertain the possibility of finding a port to hide in. Maybe he could make it into Campeche he thought, even though he knew that the Federales would most likely be there looking for him. He figured that they would most likely be at most Mexican ports within two days of Tampico and that the option of going to jail wasn't much better than that of joining the crew of sailors and smugglers at the bottom of this sea.

He was looking at the green glow of the radar display with its cluttered screen of images from the waves and rain, when he first saw it. On the screen formed an object that resembled a spider in the radar return directly in front of him. As he continued on course and the image grew larger and maintained its shape, he knew that it had to be land. The legs of the spider were fingers of land that formed two distinct bays. Bays that would give good shelter from the storm he thought, and if he could maneuver into one of them and anchor until the storm passed he would be able to continue in its lee. He set a course for the westward facing bay and headed directly towards it. He was taking an awful chance he knew. Without charts of this island to tell him the depths around it or within its bays, he was taking a large gamble to not strike a rock or reef and sink as he tried to enter. With the weather as bad as it was he would also not be able to do any kind of visual depth checks to verify his safety. The alternative of staying out in the storm was also very risky and he decided that he would have to take a chance with the harbor.

Chapter 6

Jennifer woke up with a start when her alarm went off at 6:00 a.m.. She could immediately feel that she was still very tired from staying up so late the night before talking with Michael. This and the several drinks that she had consumed throughout the night made her feel like just switching off the alarm and rolling back over for a few more hours of wonderful sleep. She quickly pulled back the covers and slid her body to the edge of the mattress so that she could put one foot on the floor. She did this little trick on a regular basis when she traveled, knowing that it would keep her from drifting back to sleep. With all that she had to do today and with her plans to meet with Michael for dinner and a beautiful sunset at Coconuts later this evening she knew that she needed to get up and get going.

Starting out her morning with her normal abdominal routine and squat thrusts, she thought about her ex-boyfriends through the years that she had reduced to whining little children as they attempted to keep up with her daily exercises. After she was through with that, she stretched her calves and hamstrings and prepared her body for a five mile run around the island that would get her day going. Jennifer had always been fanatical about her workouts. She was obsessed with her rock hard abs and really loved the added stamina that it gave her in the bedroom. Exercise was truly a labor of love for her.

Starting out from the hotel she ran down to First Street so that she would be able to run along the island's scenic seashore. As she moved along she made mental notes of the places that she wanted to return to later in the morning with her camera. These morning runs not only kept her healthy and allowed her to live and eat as she wished, they also worked very well as reconnaissance missions for the pictures that she took while traveling. She ran the entire circumference of the island, cutting in and out of back roads and back tracking where necessary since there was no road that simply ran all the way around the perimeter of the isle. She ran by the school and the tiny airport, where mechanics stood with their heads inside the engine compartment of a Cessna 172 that looked to be as old as the island itself. The runway at the airport was cracked with tall weeds growing out of it, and didn't appear to be long enough to even get a kite in the air before the flyer would go off its end and into the sea.

Jennifer wandered further into the interior along the narrow streets until she found herself at the Museum State Park near the island's north end. Here she followed the short nature trail that was there in order to change up her run a little while also taking in some of the wildlife that made this island their home. After emerging back on the road she then made her way past the school again and followed the winding road to the left until she came out by the docks that jetted out into the creeks and marsh lands that lined the main road leading back into the town. Heading back towards town now, she turned on Third Street and ran past the barnacle covered crab traps stacked along side of the road before turning right onto A Street and ending her run down by the boat ramps at the beginning of Dock Street. She looked out over the gulf water, as she wandered slowly around the parking lot cooling down from her run, and admired the boat that she had seen in the moonlight the night before. Studying the vessel which sat all alone in a quiet slumber, it took her a few moments before she noticed the movement in the water just off its back end. As she focused in on the movement she saw that there was a person in the water. Someone was really swimming out there. Not someone just bobbing around and playing in the salty gulf waters. No, someone was swimming for exercise, as if they were doing laps in an Olympic pool.

"Strange." She said aloud but to no one in particular. She had never seen anyone swimming in the open waters like this for exercise.

After watching the swimmer for a few moments she turned and headed back towards the hotel. Stopping off at the kitchen before climbing the stairs back to the second floor, she grabbed a cup of coffee and took it with her up to her room to enjoy while she got ready. She had made the decision, while she was out on her run, to wear a white cotton blouse and khaki linen shorts for the day in an attempt to stay cool in the heat that was sure to build. She had come across plenty of places where she wanted to take pictures during her earlier run and decided that her walking sandals would be the best way to beat the heat while keeping her feet comfortable through all the walking that she would definitely need to do. Setting these items out neatly on the unmade bed, Jennifer stripped from her workout clothes and headed into the small bathroom for a much needed shower.

Once she was all refreshed and ready, she checked her camera gear for all the lenses and filters that she would need for the day and grabbed two extra memory chips and an extra battery and put them in one of the side pockets of the Domke F2 camera bag. That along with the large battery pack that she already had attached to the Canon digital SLR camera body should get her through the day she figured. Jennifer grabbed the bag and headed down the stairs and out into the street.

Starting immediately, she took pictures of the old hotel with close up shots of the railings of the second floor balcony above. Moving then to the doors and windows, she wanted to get every view of this building that she could. Afterwards she walked along the sidewalk of Second Street and found many more buildings that were very old and didn't shy away from showing their age. Most of these now housed restaurants and stores that catered to the tourists in town. After taking hundreds of pictures of all of these buildings she decided to enter a gift store in one of the corner buildings and see what trinkets they had to offer.

Inside the shop Jennifer found many items sitting on the shelves as well as hanging from the ceiling. Glass sculptures that could be used as vases with hints of blues and greens painted on their surfaces. Ceramic dolls standing along the shelves with their eyes closed, silently prayed for someone to buy them. There were wooden model boats that had tiny planks of wood that were laid individually by an extremely detailed craftsman. Lines and halyards stretched down from the masts of these minute replicas, along with tiny canvas sails, to the decks below and were tied off to flawless little cleats that held them in place. Stones of all colors and sizes set into gold and silver rings and carefully displayed on steps of felt, accenting each setting to get the viewers full attention.

Jennifer stopped at a pearl that was in a black aluminum setting and hung from a leather strip necklace. It seemed very odd to her to see such a prized item like this pearl in such a rustic and simple setting.

A woman silently approached from behind her and asked, "Would you like to see something darling?"

"Yes, ma'am. May I see this pearl?" She pointed to the necklace inside the glass counter.

"Of course. Kind of a strange setting isn't it?"

"That's what I was thinking but, it's very unique and intriguing."

"My husband does those."

"Really?" Jennifer asked.

"Yes, he's an artist and sculptor and has done many of the items in here."

"They are all very lovely."

"Thank you. Here, try it on." The woman said holding the necklace up to drape over Jennifer's head. She dropped the pearl down onto Jennifer's chest and then gently tied the leather strip at the back of her neck.

"There is a mirror over on that display case. Go and see what you think."

Jennifer walked over and admired the necklace resting against her bare upper chest. She liked the way the pearl looked against her tanned skin and with the leather and black brushed aluminum body it did not look over dressy for her shorts and white summer blouse.

"I really like it," she told the woman. "It's very simple and delicate. I'll take it."

"Well, you just leave it on sweetie, and when you're ready I'll meet you over at the register."

"Thank you," Jennifer replied as she reached her hand up and flattened the gem against the skin of her chest with her fingers.

She continued looking around the store at the many items and works of art created by the woman's husband. There were many painted scenes of Cedar Key's streets and people and the marvelous sunsets. The colors were alive and vibrant on their canvases with suns that danced on tides that couldn't move. Jennifer admired these motionless images, of this small town's backdrop, that just absolutely refused to sit still.

Jennifer heard the bells above the doorway jingle as a young woman walked through the door. She had short blonde hair and was dressed in a tight tank top and shorts that said to the world, "We don't care what you think. We refuse to believe that extra thirty pounds really exists." She was talking loudly into her cell phone as she walked over to the cash register and grabbed a pack of cinnamon chewing gum from the impulse item display stand. She then pointed to the small glass doored refrigerator behind the counter and attempted to motion to the woman who had waited on Jennifer earlier, that she wanted a bottle of water as well. She did not stop her phone conversation and Jennifer overheard her telling the person on the other end of her conversation,

"I know, I know, I once burned my tongue on Chai tea so badly that I couldn't taste sushi for a month."

Sounds like an interesting conversation Jennifer thought as she walked up behind the young woman and waited in line to pay for her necklace. She watched as the blonde girl handed the woman behind the register a debit card and a five dollar bill. The woman looked back at her and then at the register which showed a total on the digital display of two dollars and thirty-four cents. Still talking on the phone the blonde was not paying much attention and was confused that the woman did not seem to be doing anything to resolve their transaction.

"I'm sorry," the blonde said. "How much is it? Yes, I think that would be a great idea."

"Two dollars and thirty-four cents," the woman responded.

"Oh, okay. Take two dollars in cash and the rest on my debit card... No, no, no, don't do that to your hair. You'll regret it for months while you grow it back."

"Thirty-four cents on debit?"

"No, put the two dollars on debit...yes, I'm telling you, you'll regret it for months."

"Okay, two dollars here," the woman stated while holding up the debit card to the blonde, "and thirty-four cents from this," holding up the five dollar bill.

"No, put it all on the debit card. Wait, I have to go. I'll call you back in a minute. I'm sorry," she said with a smile. "How much is it?"

Jennifer would normally be very annoyed standing in line behind such a person but she was in no hurry to get anywhere and was finding this whole scene to be hilarious. She watched as the two women negotiated how the payment transaction was to take place and patiently waited for her turn to pay. Once the blonde had finally paid and left, Jennifer stepped up to the register.

"Kinda like boxing with a gorilla for a minute there," she said.

"I came out with two black eyes and a broken nose I think." The woman replied.

"Well, I'll try to make this transaction a little easier on you."

"Thank you, my dear. That pearl looks absolutely divine on you."

"Thank you."

Jennifer paid for her new necklace and left the store walking out onto Second Street. Turning to her left she walked up the short hill into a neighborhood of old houses that either had been restored or were in the process of being restored. When she reached the top of the short incline that the street had made she found that the next block was all down hill to the water. Walking down the hill the street split into two separate paths that went on either side of a large oak tree and then rejoined on the other side to form the full width of the street again.

There were some small cottage style rentals along the way that looked to be very inviting for an adoring couple to stay at to get away. An older woman sat out in front in a violet painted rocking chair with a book and a cup of coffee. Jennifer and the old woman exchanged smiles and pleasantries and then both went back to their own business.

The roadway ended at the water where it intersected with G Street and Jennifer stood there for a moment, looking out to the West, over the calm sea and it's reflection of the bright azure sky above. She took in the view of the islands out on the horizon and watched the pelicans and gulls hunt from their perches on top of the wooden pilings stretching up from the depths of the water.

Taking her camera back in hand, she turned to the left and walked along the waterfront to where the street made a sharp left turn. At this corner she descended a small flight of concrete steps that lead right down into the sea. Stopping at the last step before stepping into the water she squatted down taking the camera's eye piece up so that she could spy on the world through its lens.

Concentrating first on the pelicans, she took several shots of the long billed fowl as they slowly soared high above the water looking down for a meal below the shimmering surface. Some of the pelicans playfully flew just above the water, with their wings fully spread and their feet just missing any of the small undulations in the water below.

Jennifer turned her lens as she heard a boat approaching from her left. She snapped off picture after picture of the white wooden hulled craft as it skipped along creating a wave with the V of the bow that sent the disturbed water up the hull's planks and then turned it back upon itself to delicately splash back into the clear pool below.

As the boat passed out of sight, she brought the lens back to her right where she could see the airport that she had run by earlier on the other side of the bay. She took some pictures of the newly built two story homes that lined the coast in front of the airport. Although they were painted with bright, bold island inspired colors, they just didn't seem to fit in with the rest of the buildings in the area.

The day was starting out very well for pictures. The calm Gulf waters and cloudless blue sky were making for a beautiful backdrop to all the scenery that she could take in. Jennifer went back up to the street and grabbing her equipment bag that she had left on the top step, headed up the street towards the old school.

Chapter 7

The gloomy grey clouds that stretched out to the horizon were quickly showing the darkening of the oncoming dusk. Billy knew he had to make his shot at the harbor before the darkness set in if he was to have any chance at all of making it. He was closing the distance to the mouth of the little bay quickly and was using his radar and visually watching where the waves were breaking the hardest to mark the shallow waters. Saying a little prayer he pointed the bow of the Lucille into the opening and started directly for it. The heavy following seas lifted the stern and drove the boat forward causing her to fish tail from side to side and Billy had to keep spinning the helm clockwise and then counter clockwise to keep the boat on its course. Heads of coral reef peeked through the water as the swells passed by them and Billy visually marked each one that he saw so that he knew what areas to keep clear of. He could make out the palm trees on the land swaying violently in the winds and used them to line up his entry into the bay. Staying ever attentive to the feel of his boat and the motion of the water all around her, Billy felt the control come back to him as he entered the harbor and the turbulent waters of the gulf gave way to a rolling but much more stable surface. It was dark out now and Billy was easing the Lucille to the leeward section of the bay where he would have the most protection from the violent storm. The black line of the tree tops against the dark cloudy sky was barely visible to him now as he eased up closer with what he knew was probably too much speed when. Thud!

"Shit!" He yelled aloud.

It was too late. The Lucille was aground, and while the sudden stop to all the rocking of the boat was welcome, Billy knew that he was in even more trouble now.

Chapter 8

Jennifer was in her room at the Island Hotel getting ready for her evening with Michael. She had already showered and washed away all the hours of wandering around the island that she had done. Thousands of pictures of different Gulf views, boats, old houses, buildings, docks, and wild life were uploaded to her computer now, and having accomplished what she had set out to do, she was looking forward to the night ahead. Once ready, she left her room and headed down the stairway. Stepping down from the last step Jennifer walked past the door to Neptune's Bar, through the lobby and out onto the covered sidewalk of Second Street. Feeling very confident in her size two Lucky Brand jeans and skin tight Cubby T-shirt she proudly wore her newly purchased pearl and could once again feel the heads turn her way as she walked along the sidewalk.

At Coconuts she sat back in her chair on the deck and looked out over the water at all the boats scurrying about at various speeds. She watched as the orange flaming sunset cast a shadow of the old dilapidated boat house, that sat all alone in the middle of the bay, down onto the shimmering water below it. Suddenly she was startled by a hand on her shoulder and nearly fell out of her chair as she spun around while looking up at the man standing behind her.

"Michael," she nearly screamed as her heart started to beat again.

"Hi," Michael said as he placed four Coronas on the table in front of her and acted like he hadn't seen her fervent reaction. He sat down in the other chair next to where Jennifer had been seated and calmly handed one bottle to her and took one for himself.

"Best view in town for the sunset," he said. "It's sometimes hard to get a waitress when it's this busy on the deck though." He pointed at the extra Coronas. "I find that it's always good to be prepared."

"Good that you're here to teach me these things," she responded while settling back into her seat.

"I'm here to help," he said.

As they watched the sun on its final descent for yet another day, Jennifer and Michael sat in the green plastic chairs facing off towards the western horizon and talked. Jennifer told him about her about her adventures and all the pictures that she had taken and the people that she had met as well as the sights that she had seen. Michael listened intently to all that she told him. He was really enjoying the opportunity to see this island, that he knew so well, through this virgin experience and the almost childlike enthusiasm that she had for it. He could clearly visualize all that she told him about and it almost felt like a completely new place to him as she explained what she saw through her unspoiled eyes.

As the sun set behind the boat house, the sky turned to orange with brilliant streaks of yellow and red that traced the outline of the clouds that reached out from the distant horizon. The water which was just recently a deep sparkling blue turned to a dark violet and was abruptly divided from the now glowing crimson sky by the black line of trees that made up the outer part of this island.

"Amazing." Jennifer said.

"I know." Michael said to her. "I've never been able to get enough of the sunset from here."

As the show came to its natural end with the sun completing its vanishing act Michael asked, "Are you getting hungry yet?"

"Starving," she said. "Do we need a menu?"

"Oh, we're not eating here," Michael said.

"Oh?" Jennifer was a little confused. "I just thought," was all she could get out when Michael interrupted her.

"Oh, no," Michael said. "I have a special meal planned for us this evening."

"I can hardly wait," she said.

Michael pushed back his chair and stood up. He held out his hand to Jennifer and said, "Let's go."

Jennifer stood up and they walked back from the deck and through the bar.

"Good night, Michael!" Yelled the bartender.

Michael waved over his head to the bartender and gave him a friendly nod.

Out on the street they walked by the concrete pier where fishermen were pulling in Red Fish to the delight of the pelicans swimming below. They continued along passing Frog's Landing where Jennifer had spent the previous night and then by the man with his dog who was still out selling his books. Michael finally came to a stop. He looked back to make sure that no cars were coming and then, taking Jennifer's hand they crossed the street.

Jennifer had hardly even noticed the Big Deck Raw Bar her last two times down here. It didn't have the large signs or the Gulf view like the other places. In all reality, it looked more like just another piece of the landscape. They walked inside and along the narrow walkway near the bar to emerge out on a large painted and covered deck that was open the street on one side and the little protected cove on the other. Several tables were set around the open deck and patrons sat and ate oysters and shrimp and drank their beers and rum drinks. Christmas style lights hung from the ceiling rafters giving the space a festive appearance and every table had a napkin box that held pictures of people having good times there.

Michael chose a hightop table along the back railing of the deck. From here they would be able to watch all the people at their tables living out their stories as well as look out over the little bay where people launched their boats from their trailers or tied them up to one of the small docks.

"Looks like a charming place," Jennifer said, mostly serious.

"It may not look like much, but just give it a chance," Michael replied.

The waitress came over to the table and asked, "What's it going to be, Michael?"

Jennifer gave him a curious look.

"Two Coronas, curly fries and twenty medium wings," he said. Then pausing, he looked at Jennifer. "I'm sorry, do you like wings?"

"Yes," she said with a playful smile, "but I prefer them hot."

"Twenty hot, then," he said to the waitress.

"Got it. I'll be right back with those beers." She turned and walked back to the bar and kitchen to put in their order.

"Wings and fries?" Jennifer asked.

"Just give them a chance." Michael replied to her again.

"Just wanted to be sure that I heard that right. We're on the Gulf of Mexico in one of the world's top destinations for oysters. Hundreds of choices for seafood and fish and we're having wings and fries?"

Michael just looked at her and gave her a knowing smile.

As the waitress brought out the beers, Michael was pointing at the rooftops on the buildings around the town. He showed Jennifer where the Island Hotel, Fire Station, and City Park were.

Pointing out the large barge in the middle of the bay with the heaping mounds of empty oyster shells, he explained to Jennifer, "They'll take those shells out into the Gulf and dump them. The baby oysters will later attach to them to grow."

"Really?" Asked Jennifer, "I had no idea there was more to oysters than just eating them. Never really thought about it to tell you the truth."

Michael was giving Jennifer a lesson in the proper methods of oyster diving when the waitress came over with their food order and two fresh beers. The fries were in a tight brick that was the same shape of the frying basket they had been cooked in. There must have been ten potatoes peeled, sliced and fried altogether there. Michael got up and walked over to a set of storage shelves that were along the outside of the kitchen wall and returned with a bottle of malt vinegar.

"This okay with you?" He asked as he showed her the bottle.

"Absolutely," she said.

Michael drowned the fries with the vinegar as Jennifer emptied half a bottle of ketchup on a plate to the side.

"Try one," Michael said.

Jennifer took one of the golden fried potato strings in hand and as she lifted it to her mouth her sinuses filled with the stingy aroma of the warm vinegar causing her eyes to water. She placed the fry on her tongue and let it melt in her mouth.

"Wow," was all Jennifer could say.

"Still want seafood?" Michael asked.

"No. Now I want to try one of those wings." She retorted.

She bit into one of the tender wings and immediately felt the burn of the hot sauce that she expected from them. The thing that caught her taste buds by surprise though, was the flavor she tasted immediately after the burn. They seemed to have a familiar smoky taste.

"Grilled wings?" She asked.

"That's correct." Michael responded.

"What is this place?" Jennifer asked in astonishment.

"Like I said, just give it a chance." Michael smiled at her as he grabbed a wing and put it in his mouth.

After they enjoyed the meal, along with several more Coronas to wash down the heat of the spicy red sauce, Michael paid the bill and they got up and left.

They walked down the street until it opened up to the Gulf. Jennifer took Michael's hand and said to him, "I'm having a great evening." She hesitated for a second and then looking out to the Gulf she saw the anchored boat again and changed the subject.

"Some people really know how to live."

Michael looked out to where she was looking.

"The boat?" He asked. "That's the Lucy."

"You know that boat?" She seemed a little surprised.

"Sure do. That's my boat. I live on it."

Jennifer drew back with a little shock. The fact that this was Michael's boat wasn't really a surprise to her so much as that after talking for a couple hours the night before and the few hours together tonight, she didn't know the first things about him. She thought about their conversations together. He was always asking questions about her. He was interested in her. This seemed so foreign and strange. She always seemed to listen to the guys she knew go on and on about themselves and sports and whatever else. Who was this guy? Wait a minute, she thought, who *is* this guy?

Suddenly she was running over the past twenty-four hours. What kind of position had she put herself in? She thought about him in the bar at the hotel and in the swing on the balcony. The bartenders all seemed to know him. He was probably a local. This made her feel a little better. Need to find out more about him, she thought, or do I? I am leaving tomorrow after all. Maybe a quick fling would be exactly what I need. She stopped her thought when she realized that Michael was looking at her. Was he talking to her?

"Sorry," she said realizing the moment had become awkward. "That's your boat?"

"Yes," he said. "I live on it," he proclaimed again.

"So you're a local here?"

"Not really," he said. "I come here on my boat for supplies and things but I don't live around here."

He took her by the hand and they walked over to the gazebo at the City Park. They sat on the bench inside the gazebo looking out over the beach and Jennifer reluctantly told Michael that she needed to leave the next day.

"Where to?" He asked.

"Apalachicola."

"Really? They have the best oysters there. I would love to take you. I was heading out tomorrow anyway. Let me take you."

"Take me? On the boat?"

"Yes," Michael said. "It'll be fun."

She was not looking forward to driving all the way to Apalachicola alone and this would mean that she could spend a few more days with Michael too.

"I don't want to be a burden or anything."

"Not at all. I haven't been there in a while and I've been meaning to go. You're helping me out by giving me an excuse."

Jennifer thought about it for a minute.

"I'd really love that, but I don't even know you."

"What's there to know?" He said, and then seeing the concern in her face, he continued. "You can ask about me. Most people on this island know who I am. I've been around here for quite a few years. I used to live here and bartend a few years back."

"I did notice that quite a few people here know you by name."

"You have nothing to worry about with me, Jennifer. I will be the perfect gentleman."

"I don't know if all that would be necessary." She said.

"Great then. We'll leave tomorrow. I'll come up to the hotel in the morning to get you."

Jennifer could only smile at him.

It was getting late now and Michael and Jennifer decided to part ways for the evening to get some sleep. Jennifer went back to her room at the Island Hotel and Michael went out to his boat. He stayed up for another hour getting a few things ready for the next day, and then picked up his copy of Herman Wouk's book to help settle his mind before heading off for some much needed sleep.

Chapter 9

Billy had only gotten a few hours of sleep before he woke up with a start. He sat up straight and it took a few cloudy minutes for him to realize that he was onboard the Lucille on the small couch that was in the pilot house. Slowly he started to remember the night before. He remembered that he had checked the interior of the boat for damage and then looked through his cargo for anything broken down there. In the rain and wind of the previous night it was hard to see the land clearly but he had estimated it to be about seventy-five yards or so out from where he sat aground. "Why did you get so close?" He had argued with himself.

Now it was morning. The rain had stopped and the wind had subsided to what he figured to be about fifteen miles per hour now. He would be able to get a good look at the boat this morning and start working on getting himself back out to sea and then home to his wife.

As he stood up and looked out the windows, he could see the trees that lined the edge of the beach very clearly now. Something seemed to be missing though. Billy stood there looking at the palm trees swaying in the wind and then at all the branches and leaves lying about the beach. He walked out onto the deck in disbelief as he looked at the wet sand continue all the way from the tree line to his boat and then out on the other side of the hull where he could finally see the small waves crashing down into the sand and then pulling back out to the bay. This was much worse than he had feared. Not only was he run aground in the bay, but when the storm surge brought on by Tropical Storm Candy subsided, it left him helplessly stranded on the beach.

Securing his rope ladder and throwing it over the side, Billy climbed down the precarious steps to the beach below. He immediately set out to begin a thorough check of the hull, shafts and propellers. His inspection was quickly cut short when he saw that the V of the hull had dug deeply into the sand from the speed that he had been going when he hit and it was nearly impossible to see what damage the propeller and shafts had taken since they were mostly buried in the white sand of the beach. Billy fell back onto his butt in the sand and looked at the wooden hulled structure rising up in front of him. It looked almost like a beach house just sitting there waiting for someone to move in.

"What am I going to do?" He said aloud to himself. "What can I possibly do?"

Chapter 10

The next morning Michael got up and went for a twenty minute swim in the harbor to wake up. He had always kept himself in great physical condition and he loved how living on a boat made a morning swim always available to him. When he was finished he showered and threw on a T-shirt and cargo shorts before he hopped into his skiff and headed to shore. He was very excited about getting underway today since he had been in Cedar Key a week longer than he intended and was ready to go. He was also excited that he was taking Jennifer to Apalachicola so that he would be able to spend some more time with her before he headed back home.

Walking up to the Island Hotel he could see Jennifer sitting in a chair on the balcony.

She waved and yelled down to him, "Grab some coffee and come on up."

"Don't mind if I do," he replied.

Michael grabbed himself a cup of coffee from the kitchen of the hotel's restaurant and headed up the stairs into the large sitting room at the top and then out onto the balcony where Jennifer sat in an adirondack chair with her own cup of joe.

"Good morning," he said to Jennifer as he passed through the door.

"Good morning." She replied. "What time are we going to get going?"

"As quick as we can." He said. " I need to run into the mainland for a few supplies for the boat and we can return your rental car while we are there."

"Excellent," Jennifer said. "I was sitting up here this morning trying to figure out how to get the car back. That will be perfect. Thank you."

"Why don't you get all your stuff packed and check out? I'm going to head over to my friend's place by the airport to borrow his Jeep."

"Okay," she said, "I need to shower and get ready, too. Meet back here in about an hour then?"

"Perfect," Michael said.

Michael made the walk over to his friends house in less than half an hour and found the Jeep parked along side the palm tree in the front yard. It was an older CJ that had absolutely no frills at all. A Bimini top that kept the sun from shining directly down on the driver and passenger was the only accessory afforded for this rugged little four by four. The three speed transmission and short wheelbase gave the vehicle a ride that was just a little superior to riding in a horse and buggy along a rocky mountain road. Michael found the keys sitting where his friend had left them under an overturned half coconut shell on his back porch. With a single turn of the key in the ignition, the trustworthy six cylinder engine roared to life. He drove it out into the street and headed over to the local gas station to fill up the tank before heading over to the Island Hotel to get Jennifer. She was standing out on the sidewalk with her bags when he arrived. Tossing the bags into the back of the Jeep she then hopped into her rental car and followed him into the small farming town of Chiefland. This small community on the mainland was the nearest place for her to turn in the rental car. While she was doing that, Michael ran to the hardware and grocery stores and bought the supplies that he needed. Once he was done, he picked up Jennifer and they headed back to Cedar Key.

At the docks, they loaded Jennifer's bags and the supplies into the skiff and started out to Michael's boat.

"What about your friend's Jeep?" Jennifer asked.

"He's going to pick it up at the dock later," Michael responded. "He was coming down to the dock for dinner tonight anyway."

Michael turned the skiff towards the tiny bridge that spanned the narrow opening for the harbor and within minutes of clearing the little channel he had her up on a plane as they went around the concrete fishing pier and headed out to the Lucy.

The Lucy was a beautiful fifty foot Hatteras Motor Yacht. The sleek painted white lines of her hull, and modern luxuries from Michael's refits over the years for comfort and appearance, did wonders to hide her 1968 date of birth. He had also updated the radar and navigation equipment with the latest technology so that he would never have a problem with handling the boat by himself as he travelled.

Jennifer climbed the starboard side ladder ahead of Michael and took the supplies and bags as he passed them up to her. She then placed them inside the boat's pilot house to get them out of the way before heading inside to explore. Meanwhile, Michael had maneuvered the little skiff around to the stern of the boat and attached it to the boom and winch system that would lift it into its place on the upper deck. Moving through the spacious cabin Jennifer immediately noticed that Michael was either a very neat and organized man or he had spent some quality time cleaning the boat before she arrived today. Either way, she liked it.

She looked at the decor of the boat and found that it was hard to tell what Michael's personality really was from the items that he had about. There was a large flat screen TV attached to one wall of the saloon, which she fully expected to see, and then across from it was a painting by Salvador Dali that appeared to be two men thinking, or two hands pointing, or some combinations of the two. The entire boat was decorated with fine collections of leather bound books and what had to be hundreds of pictures of different people, that looked like they must be friends of his, in well polished antique frames. The boats steering wheel was a heavily varnished teak wood with brightly shined brass hardware all around its circumference, and the instruments and displays on the control panel looked to be brand new and completely automated giving the interior space a digital glow that contrasted very nicely with the old fashioned styling of everything else.

Jennifer heard Michael start the twin diesel engines of the Lucy as he prepared her to get underway. After taking her things and putting them in the forward cabin she came out onto the deck to find him.

"Is there anything that I can do to help?" She asked.

"I have it under control," Michael responded and then as an afterthought he stated. "In truth, I could really use a beer."

"Where are they?"

"The fridge on the back deck is stocked," he said.

"I'm on my way."

As Jennifer grabbed two Coronas from the fridge, she saw some limes in a small hammock hanging over the wet bar. He thinks of everything, she thought to herself.

Michael moved the boat ahead slowly and used a remote to control the anchor winch from the cockpit. It was essential for anyone who navigated a boat of this size by themselves to have any convenience that they could get to make their lives a little easier. Once the anchor was securely in its hold, Michael returned to the other gauges of the cockpit and eased the boat out of the harbor and out into the open waters of the Gulf of Mexico. He sat forward in his captan's chair and using the dials to the right side of his throttles, set a course for Apalachicola. After making sure that the course was properly set, he took a drink of his beer and looked over at Jennifer who was sitting on a bench seat to his left.

"And, we're off." He said.

Jennifer smiled and looked out ahead of the boat at the dark blue water and crisp blue sky with its few fluffy white clouds floating above. I can't believe that I was going to drive there, she thought.

"This is beautiful," she said aloud.

"Absolutely is," Michael replied.

They sat in silence for a while taking in the view and breathing in the clean fresh air. The boat rolled along the top of the gentle swells with a smooth yet powerful force. They could feel themselves being pushed back into their seats from the power of the engines while they were gently rocked like a little babies by the water's motion. The heat of the day was beating down now and Jennifer really wanted to get some warm sun on her.

She looked at Michael, "Would you mind if I take in a little sun for a while?"

"Go right ahead," Michael replied. "The view stays exactly like this for a while."

"Great," she said.

Jennifer went down below and changed into her azure green Victoria's Secret bikini. She went out onto the boat's rear deck and laid out on her stomach on the cushioned couch that ran the width of the back of the boat. She undid the straps to her top and let them fall down off the edges of the couch. The sun's heat beating down on her completely bare back felt great as the tiny beads of sweat started to build. Letting herself become completely relaxed with the warm sun, the gentle roll of the gulf and the constant hum of the diesel engines, she started to fall asleep.

After a short while, Michael who had worked up a thirst by cleaning the upper pilot house, came down the ladder into the rear deck. He turned and saw Jennifer lying there with her bare back being tanned by the burning Gulf sun.

"Need another beer?" He asked.

Jennifer was a bit startled and looked over at Michael.

Calmly, she asked, "Umm Michael? Who's steering the boat?"

Michael laughed, "Auto helm has it."

"Auto helm? Ah, very good." Jennifer responded, as if she had some idea of what he had just said to her, and then laid her head back down.

"Need another beer?" Michael asked again.

"Oh, yes," she replied. "That would be perfect."

Michael brought her over a Corona with lime. He couldn't take his eyes off of the long slender lines of her thin torso. He could see the short blonde hairs of her back as they seemingly reached up to the sun in praise from her soft tan skin.

"Here you go," Michael said, holding the beer out to her as he walked up.

"Thank you," Jennifer said as she turned to Michael and reached out exposing the side of her breast. Michael blushed a little as he looked up from his short stare and noticed that she was smiling at him.

"I'll be back up at the helm." He said.

"Okay, I'll be up in a little bit."

"Need anything else before I go?"

"No thanks, I'm good."

"Okay then, I'll see you in a little bit."

"Okay." Jennifer smiled widened as she watched his uneasiness. She turned her head and again laid it back down. This little trip was going in all the right directions.

Chapter 11

"Ricotta, Ricotta, Ricotta, this is Agave, do you copy? Over. Ricotta, Ricotta, Ricotta, this is Agave, do you copy? Over."

Billy had been calling out on the preplanned frequency for over two hours now. Breaking for five minutes after every five minutes of hailing, right on the set schedule. Finally, to his relief, the response came.

"Agave, Agave, this is Ricotta. I copy. Over."

"Ricotta, it's great to hear you. Thank God."

"Mister Sanchez, how are you? We were very worried."

"I am good, Ricotta. Boat problems, but good. How is Mrs. Sanchez?"

"Mrs. Sanchez and bebe are A-OK señor."

Billy sat back in the captain's chair and wiped away the tear that had just formed in the outer corner of his eye.

"Bebe?" He asked quite startled, "Niña or niño?"

"Miguel."

"Miguel." Billy replied.

He was very sad that he had missed the birth of his son. He knew that he had broken the promise that he had made to his beautiful wife. He felt like a total failure. He had disappointed his soul mate, and missed one of the greatest moments of their lives. He longed now, more than ever, to be home with his family.

"Ricotta," Billy said in a very somber voice, "I am in trouble. I need some assistance."

"Agave, just let me know what you need and where you are. Whatever you need."

"Twenty clicks south of the Mason Dixon." he said to him. "One thousand clicks from Terra Firma.

Billy and his brother Patrick had worked out a series of secret passwords and call signs years before so that they could openly communicate on the radio with minimum concern about who might be listening in. The Mason Dixon was the East West line that they ran through the Gulf from Tampico, Mexico to their home port in Key Largo, Florida which was known as Terra Firma. Ricotta was the emergency call sign used to contact the opposite brother whenever they found themselves in any kind of trouble. Whatever they used as their own call sign when calling out Ricotta, denoted the last or current location of the one calling. Agave, which Billy was using now, told his brother that he had just left Tampico. It was a simple code and by using chief ingredients of the cargo that they received from each port, agave for tequila from Mexico, tobacco for the cigars from Cuba and cane for the rum from Hispanola, there wasn't a lot of confusion.

"Copy, Agave. What needs do you have?"

"Not sure yet. I'm still assessing the situation. High and dry right now. Rope and cargo space would be a good start."

"Copy, Agave. I will be on my way soon. Assess and advise as you can."

"Copy, Ricotta. Agave out."

Billy took a minute to think about his wife and newly born son. He quickly recovered from his defeatist thoughts and began on a plan to get himself home to them. His brother would be on his way to him soon and would be there to get him in just a few days. Worst case, they could transfer their cargo of bootlegged rum and tequila to Patrick's boat and abandon his poor Lucille where she lie.

He climbed back down the ladder to the beach and started out to the tree line to investigate the tiny island. He had plenty of supplies on the boat to last until his brother arrived so he had no worries there, but he knew that it is always best to know your surroundings and what assets the land might provide if needed. As he walked along the line of trees at the edge of the beach he looked into the thick foliage for any paths or fruit trees or anything else that he could possibly use. Moving along and looking deep he saw what at first appeared to be a field of grass on the other side of the palms and palmettos and then after further investigation he saw that it was actually water on the other side of the dense vegetation. Carefully, he cleared a trail using his machete and made his way over to the water.

As he came to the edge of it he could now see that it was the other bay that he had clearly seen on the radar screen during the previous nights storm. The dark, clear water did not seem to have a bottom to it and the edges, in contrast to the beach where his boat sat sunning itself, was made up of rock cliffs that rose twenty feet or more at points and dropped straight down into the calm black water. He could see that there were Coconut and Mango tress mixed with Cuban Laurels lining the banks of the tops of these cliffs. I'll need to climb that hill and see what else is up there, he thought to himself.

This bay had dark water that stretched east all the way out into the Gulf. He knew immediately that this would be a good spot for his brother to pull his boat into when he arrived. Billy made plans to start clearing the area where he was now, which was right at sea level, so that they could tie his boat there. Looking straight down the edge of the rock into the water he knew that he could clearly see twenty or more feet down with no bottom in sight.

From there he climbed the hill to the North side of the island, clearing as much of the foliage as he could as he went. The thick brush quickly dulled his long knife as he went and he started to just step his way through the hard ground cover. He was making good time up the hill and was looking forward to a wonderfully sweet ripe mango from the trees at the top when suddenly it was dark all around him. It had happened so fast and unexpectedly that he still didn't have any of his senses about him. And then, as if on some sort of cue, the pain started to set in. It started in his back and then spread out to his limbs and head. He felt more of a soreness in his muscles than a sharp pain as he slowly moved each body part one by one. He then began to get his sense of smell back as a putrid and damp odor filled his sinus cavity. He sat in the darkness trying to focus on anything when he realized that there was a faint light all around him. Actually, as he researched the faint light around him he saw that there was a more focused light off to his left. Looking up he finally saw the source of the faint light as he focused on the large hole in the rocks above him. He began to remember now, the loss of balance as he pushed through some palmetto leaves and the sudden and violent stop as his body made its crushing contact with the ground below.

Slowly he maneuvered to get onto his hands and knees so that he would be able to stand up. His night vision was starting to come to him but it was still extremely dark all around. Beneath his hands he could feel the cold damp floor of the cave with the slimy mud that covered it's solid rock. Pushing against the floor with his arms, he rocked back from his knees onto his feet and stood up. He looked towards the focused circle of light that he had noticed earlier and began to walk toward it.

Getting closer to the cave's opening he was beginning to see all around himself better as the light filtered in and the mouth of the cave opened up to a large hollow chamber before spilling back out into daylight on the beach of the western bay. Before going out to the beach, Billy looked around the large chamber. The ground was covered by bat droppings which made him immediately look up to see if he could see any of the free hanging nocturnal creatures. He did not see any bats hanging there but did instead see several cylindrical holes through the rock leading to the sky above. Looking back into the shadows from where he had come, he noticed now that there were several other caves that lead off from this main opening and into the rocky and dark unknown.

Billy walked out into the glaring daylight, down the beach and directly into the clear, salty water. Wading out until he was soaked up to his waist he fell backwards saturating his entire body and then began lightly scrubbing with his hands to get all the dirt and guano off of him. Standing back on his feet he looked over at the Lucille and her high comfortable perch on the sand. He felt a sadness for his boat, seeing it just sitting there helpless and unable to do anything to save herself. She just laid there still without even a struggle or a sigh. Billy stripped out of his dirty soaked clothes and bundled them all together so that he could easily carry them. Staying in the comforting warm water he swam over toward where his boat sat on the beach. He waded naked through the surf and climbed the ladder up to the boat's deck and started toward his stateroom to get some fresh clothes. With his first step he heard a loud agonizing creaking noise that closely resembled the scream of a young child, followed by the deck unexpectedly moving downward by at least a foot and then a thunderous *crack*.

Billy knew immediately that something terribly life altering had just happened. He stood there still for a moment to be sure that the boat was done moving and then quickly he made his way into his stateroom and grabbed some shorts and a T-shirt and then he was up and over the side and down to the beach below to examine the boat again.

Once on the beach he could see the damage that had just happened. The back end of the boat was now sitting down lower into the sand. Somewhere around the midpoint of the vessel's deck there was a distinct contortion in the wood hull's lines and then an angled downward slope as he looked at her from the side. Some of the boards of the hull in this area were bulging or completely split. The keel of the aging craft had completely given way and broken. Probably under the extreme weight of the numerous bottles of liquid that made up her cargo along with the beating that she had taken from the sea the previous day. The Lucille was now finished and it was time for her captain to abandon ship.

Chapter 12

It only took a few hours to get the Lucy across the short stretch of Gulf water and through the Saint George Sound into Apalachicola Bay. Steering the Hatteras under the John Gorrie Memorial Bridge they ran up the Apalachicola River and tied up to the piers that were out in front of Boss Oyster's. This was Michael's favorite bar and restaurant in this city and he loved that he could dock right out in front of it. The rickety old dock had taken some damage from all of the storms through the years and required a sure foot and a brave heart to venture out onto it. Michael ran hoses and the lines for water and electricity to the Lucy before going below for a much needed shower. Jennifer immediately got on her cell phone to let her employer know that she had arrived in town.

After getting ready, Jennifer and Michael went up to Boss Oyster and had a seat on the old deck near the railing. From here they could look out past the Lucy and see the river with its tied up shrimp boats along the shoreline as well as the sailboats that were anchored out on the far side of the river. They ordered two Coronas and a dozen raw oysters from the waitress to get their evening started.

"I spoke to my boss," Jennifer told Michael. It felt odd to her to refer to someone as her boss since she had been self employed for years now.

"Yeah?" Michael replied. "Is he meeting you here?"

"Tomorrow morning," she said. "Down at the Consulate."

"Very beautiful place."

"I haven't seen it yet, but from what I know of Douglas it would have to be."

A large silver serving plate topped with ice and the twelve shucked oysters on the half shell arrived and was set between them. They worked through these quickly as Michael ordered a variety of specialty oyster dishes from the menu. Some with jalepeno and cheese, some with bacon and hot sauce. The beers kept coming as they sat and talked about their quick trip up here and their past few days in Cedar Key. Much had happened in a few short days and they were not ready to slow down or go their separate ways yet. They talked and laughed as they ate their dinner and continued with more cervezas. Jennifer started feeling the alcohol go to her head and decided that she needed to get back to the boat.

"We better get back out to the boat while I can still walk right," Jennifer said. Then after thinking about what she had just said, she added "Oh my God. Is it okay that I stay on the boat tonight? I didn't even think about getting a room somewhere."

"That's fine," Michael said. "I expected you to stay on board tonight."

"I'm so embarrassed that I didn't even think twice." She paused, "Wait a minute" she said. "You expected me to stay on board?"

"Don't read into that Jennifer. I just expected that you would stay," he paused, "in your cabin."

"Thanks," Jennifer said a little more calmly now. "Ready to head back?"

"Let's go."

Once back on the Lucy Jennifer sat on the back covered deck while Michael went and made them a couple of dirty martinis.

"Three olives," Michael said as he handed one to Jennifer.

"Thank you," she replied. "What do you do for a living, Michael?"

"I own a bar," he said.

"Really? Anywhere that I would know?"

"No, I really doubt you've heard of it. It's kind of a 'locals only' spot."

"Sounds like my kind of place."

"We really get some interesting characters there."

"Will you take me there some time?"

"We may be able to work out a deal," Michael said.

Jennifer gave him a sly look after that remark and took a sip of her martini.

"I think I'm going to head down to bed now," Jennifer said. "Too much fresh air, sun, and alcohol."

"Okay," Michael replied. "Take the cabin that your things are in."

Michael watched as she walked inside the saloon and up to her cabin. He took another sip of his martini and leaning back in his chair, he thought about his friends back at the bar. It had been weeks since he had last been there. It was time for him to go home.

Chapter 13

Billy had cleared much of the underbrush that was closest to the deep blue water of the East bay in just a few short hours. He was working with a very deliberate diligence now because he knew that it was not safe to be onboard the Lucille, and he would desperately need some shelter before nightfall. His only breaks from removing shrubs and long grass were used to sharpen his machete for the next round of hacking away at the foliage again.

As he worked his way from the straight rock edge where the land met the water, he noticed a cut out in the cliff wall that rose up from the water and formed the North hill where he had fallen into the cave earlier in the day. He made his way over by moving along an overgrown shelf of land and discovered the opening to yet another cave hidden behind some fanning giant ferns. This opening was approximately six feet high and just as wide and as he passed through he was very surprised to see that it opened up to a large cavern that appeared to go back into the rock about one hundred feet. The floor of the cave was smooth cold rock and seemed to rise as he walked deeper into its darkness. The light was very limited in the back recesses of the large room but he was able to make out a smaller hole in the back wall where light seemed to be coming in. He went over to the hole and made his way through and into another chamber that was better lit. Looking up he saw that there were large holes above that were letting the light in. He followed another path from this room and eventually found himself in the same large chamber that opened widely onto the western beach and bay that he had been in earlier.

Walking back out to the beach, he looked over at the Lucille as she sat hunched on the beach now. I will have to move into that cave by the East bay, he thought to himself. I can leave most of the bushes in front of the opening to help protect me from the weather. He started back along the beach toward the clearing that he had made and taking his machete back in hand worked to clear a space in the direction of the opening.

As the sun was closing the gap to the horizon Billy went onto the Luceille and retrieved a few things that he would need for the evening. Some food and blankets and warmer clothes as the temperature would most definitely fall in the darkness. Matches to build a fire that he could cook by and also use to generate some heat in the later evening. He was also sure to grab a bottle of rum from the cargo hold. He had worked hard today and he felt that he had earned it.

With a fire of the bushes and trees that he had cleared during the day blazing on the beach, Billy sat on the sand and watched one of the most spectacular sunsets that he had ever seen. Being a sailor he had seen many days end with an orange flaming ball of light fizzling out into the waters of the horizon. This sunset though, with the clouds of the storm dissipating as the sky turned yellow and orange above them, was unequalled due to the foreground of aqua colored waters and the dark patches on the surface caused by the coral below. The two lonely palm trees at the mouth of the bay framed the sun between them perfectly guiding the sun to the horizon.

Chapter 14

Jennifer woke up slowly around 10 a.m.. She rolled over in the bunk and looked at the time on her cell phone and then thought to herself in a near panic, wow I never sleep this late. After she realized that the world didn't end while she took in a few extra hours of sleep, she had a revelation that it felt great. She laid in bed while she was waking up and looked at the cabin around her. It was a very lovely room with an abundance of wood and pictures of islands and all sorts of people having fun. Not store bought pictures of other people's boats and fancy nautical phrases, but much more personal shots of real people and real places. She wondered if Michael had taken these photos.

As she sat up on the berth she started to think about her plans for the day. She was scheduled to meet with Douglas at his room at The Consulate at noon. He wanted to see the pictures that she had taken in Cedar Key. It seemed now like months had gone by since she had met with Douglas in Jacksonville. It felt like ages since George had approached her with this job while she sat with her martini lunch at the Coq d'Or in Chicago.

Chicago... She had all but forgotten about her adopted hometown. Her studio, and her friends had all slipped her mind over the past few days. She had allowed herself to get so lost in the Florida Panhandle and the time that she was spending with Michael that she had just let everything go. She made a mental note to call her assistant Shelby at the studio as soon as she could and see how things were going.

Michael was sitting on the back deck of the Lucy with his feet propped up on the side rail when she came out from her cabin. He was drinking his second cup of coffee for the morning and gazing out over the Apalachicola River. He watched the floating conveyor of fishing boats running up and down the calm morning waters. The hard working men on the decks of each of the vessels that came by would take a moment of their time to give a friendly wave and smile as they passed.

"Beautiful morning," Jennifer said from behind him.

"Absolutely is," Michael replied. "There's coffee in the galley."

"Already grabbed a cup," Jennifer said as she raised the cup in her hands.

"Very good," he said. "Have a seat."

Jennifer sat in the chair along the port side of the boat and looked over at Michael.

"I have to meet with my boss's partner at noon over at The Consulate."

"That's just up the road a few blocks from here."

"Good. I was wondering where exactly I was going to be heading."

They sat and talked some morning pleasantries for a few minutes and then Jennifer stood up.

"I need to shower and get ready."

"Okay,' Michael said. "I'll make us a little breakfast while you do that. Omelette?"

"That sounds terrific. I'm starving, thanks."

Jennifer went off to get ready and Michael went into the galley to prepare his favorite breakfast concoction.

"An omelette," Michael said aloud so that Jennifer could hear him in her cabin as she was getting ready, "is one of man's greatest food inventions. How else can you enjoy fresh vegetables along with yesterday's leftovers and fight a hangover all at the same time?"

Michael had gone through the refrigerator and found some onions, peppers and mushrooms. He had some diced chicken leftover from when he had made a stir fry a few days ago and some gravy in a jar that he had bought when he ran to the store in Chiefland. After sauteing the onions and peppers in a small yellow sea of butter, he combined them with the mushrooms and chicken until everything was heated through. He then added the gravy and let it simmer as he whisked some eggs in a mixing bowl and then poured them into a heated frying pan.

"The first secret to getting a great omelette is to completely beat your eggs until they form one uniform color and get as much air into the mixture as you can to make them fluffy. The second secret is to flip the eggs over once before adding your other ingredients so that you cook the eggs through."

Michael flipped the eggs over in the pan and then immediately added shredded cheese to the slightly browned side of them to get it melting. He then put about half of the chicken and mushroom sauce on top of the cheese and folded half of the circular shaped egg up and over to make a yellow half moon with cheese and chicken and mushroom gravy oozing out of the sides. Sliding it onto a plate he then poured the rest of the gravy on top of the omelette and then sliced one half of it onto another plate to give to Jennifer.

"Bon appetite." He told Jennifer as she came in and sat at the island bar in the galley.

"Looks delicious." She said.

"Your eyes do not deceive you. Enjoy."

Jennifer took her fork and cutting into her portion of the omelette she dipped it into the gravy to ensure a good smothering of the vegetable chicken mixture and took a bite.

"Wow. You really do know how to make a breakfast."

"Wait until I make you dinner." He gave her a little smile.

"Is that another date?" She asked.

"Yes, I believe it is." He said. "We'll set a time and day once you get back from your meeting."

"I can't wait." Jennifer said as she stuck her fork back into her food.

Once she had finished eating, Jennifer headed up to The Consulate to meet with Douglas. As she walked up the street she could see that he was sitting out on the large upper deck that went the full length of the front of the building watching for her. She admired the all brick facade of the hotel with its white doors and trim. The black steel balustrades, rails and columns eloquently blending in with the brick steps and walls. A single sign hung high over the center steps stating, "The Grady Market." She could see the history in this building. It had been carefully refurbished to have modern updates without losing its style.

Douglas waved down to Jennifer.

"Come on up," he yelled down. "It's the single door to the right of the sign."

Jennifer walked up the stairs and into Douglas's suite at The Consulate. The Ambassador, as the suite was known, was over 1600 square feet of living space. The weathered brick walls gave a colonial feel to the main room. The white kitchen cupboards and appliances with the grey concrete countertops were contrasting to the old aged feel to the room, but the square glass fronts of the cupboard doors tied the older feeling back into the room perfectly. The entire room had knotty pine wood floors with rugs under tables and chairs. The room gave off a feeling of money and comfort and Jennifer was completely mesmerized by all of it.

Douglas showed her to the sitting area and Jennifer set her laptop on the small coffee table as she sat in one of the thickly cushioned chairs.

"Very delightful place." Jennifer said.

"I like to come here from time to time," Douglas responded. "Like to come to this area for some peace and quiet and to overindulge on the wonderful oysters."

"Definitely a great place for that," she said.

"Did you bring some pictures for me to see?"

Right to business, Jennifer thought to herself. Just as well, the sooner she was done the sooner she could get back to Michael.

Jennifer opened her laptop and brought up the pictures that she had taken in Cedar Key.

"Very beautiful area," Jennifer said referring to Cedar Key in the pictures as she turned the laptop to Douglas. She showed him how to navigate through the pictures and sat back in her chair as he hunched over the screen and poured through the pictures. Jennifer watched as he flipped through picture after picture seemingly looking for something specific rather than looking at the beauty of the area to see if he and George would like to invest in the area.

Douglas continued scrolling through the shots and then suddenly, he stopped on a single picture. Jennifer watched as he sat upright with a smile on his face and looked across the small table at her.

"Excellent," he said. "You did an excellent job here."

Jennifer looked at him puzzled. What was he looking at? A piece of property with a view? A restaurant or bar?

Douglas stood up and looked at Jennifer.

"Excuse me for a moment please," he said. "I need to make a phone call."

Douglas walked out onto the deck dialing his cell phone. As the door closed behind him, Jennifer could clearly hear him say to the person on the other end, "She found it."

Jennifer stood up and walked around the table to see that the picture that was still on the screen of her computer was one of Michael's boat, The Lucy. How very odd she thought. Just then Douglas came back in and said, "Would you like a drink, Jennifer?"

She stared at him with a curious look on her face. Had he just jumped down the two stairs coming down into the room from outside? He looked almost childlike in his movements now.

"Vodka tonic?" She asked.

"Coming right up." He beamed.

Douglas went into the kitchen and took out two crystal tumblers. He added ice and then two shots of vodka and topped off with tonic water and lime.

"Here you go," he said. "Let's go out on the deck and enjoy them. It's a beautiful day."

Chapter 15

Michael was walking along the boardwalk on the Apalachicola River. He loved to walk past the all shrimp boats with their booms and rigging pulled up and pointing straight to the sky. The thick and pungent smell of the sea was quite potent here and a familiar smell to him that reminded him of home.

The nails in the boards of the boardwalk were loose in areas which allowed slight amounts of movement and the sound of creaking lumber under Michaels feet. Looking out over the river he could see the pelicans as they flew about and practiced their bombing dives into the murky water. Michael loved to watch pelicans anytime that he saw them. Such an amazing bird to see swimming close by, with those big thoughtful eyes watching from behind those long slender beaks. With their mandibles dipped slightly into the water they will study you with those pensive eyes and mark your every move so that they can continuously plot their eventual escape.

As Michael walked along the waterfront he could see The Consulate off to his right. The current owners had done such a marvelous job refurbishing this gorgeous building and had turned it into the one of the nicest places in town. Nearly one hundred years had gone by since it's heyday as the French consulate's headquarters when Apalachicola was one of the busiest ports in the Gulf of Mexico.

Michael looked over at the old brick building with its white trim and doors along with the black railings. Above the center doors of the building hanging from the railings of the porch above was the sign that said, "The Grady Market." He hesitated for a moment as he saw someone who looked very familiar to him sitting in one of the wooden adirondack chairs on the upper porch. As a slow recognition took place in his mind, Michael went into a state of shock and tried to run but couldn't move his legs. Staring in disbelief at this person sitting there above that sign, he was beginning to regain his ability to think when he noticed that Jennifer was sitting there too.

"Jennifer," he said aloud to himself. "Jennifer," he said again.

Why was she up there sitting and having a drink with Douglas Wilson?

Michael turned his head and began walking quickly south towards The Lucy.

How could Jennifer have deceived him like that? How could they have found him? He thought that he was rid of them for good and had mistakenly let down his guard. Michael picked up the pace, almost breaking into a run. Had they seen him there? He had to get out of Apalachicola right now. How did they find him?

Chapter 16

Jennifer sat out on the deck with Douglas enjoying her drink and the warm sunlight. Douglas was asking her questions about the pictures. He wanted to know exactly where she was when she had taken them. When exactly she had taken them. He seemed less interested, or even not interested at all in her taking any more pictures along the Florida coastline now. He was very excited about what she had already done.

After a while Jennifer told Douglas that she needed to go. She told him that she was meeting with a friend for dinner and she needed to go and get ready. Douglas showed her back downstairs and waved very gentlemanly as she headed south on Water Street towards Michael and The Lucy. What a strange meeting that had been she thought. She figured that she would be giving a progress report and then getting a new assignment from Douglas as to where to go and take more pictures. Instead she had the feeling that she was done now and was about to be given a ticket back to Chicago.

As Jennifer walked through Boss Oyster and outside to where the Lucy was docked, she could see that Michael was very busy up on her decks.

"Hey Michael." Jennifer yelled up to him.

Michael turned, alarmed, and then she saw a very different look on his face. Something Jennifer had not seen in him yet. Was he angry?

"What do you want?" was all that Michael could say.

"What?" She replied, a bit startled by his attitude. "What do you mean?"

"You can get your things. I already set them on the back deck."

"Michael," she said. "What's wrong? What happened?"

"You've been playing me. How could you do that?"

"Playing you? What do you mean?"

"I saw you. I saw you with him."

"Who?" Jennifer was confused by all this and was starting to feel hurt by Michael's tone.

"Don't play around with me," Michael said to her. "Please get your things. Because of you I have to get going right now."

"No! I want you to explain to me what you are talking about."

Michael had started the engines and was making his way around to retrieve the mooring lines.

"Look," he said. "I have to get underway right now and you need to get off this boat!"

"Michel, I don't know what is wrong but I am not getting off this boat until we talk."

With the lines now untied from the pilings and lying on the Lucy's deck, Michael went back up to the bridge with Jennifer following right behind him.

"Well, I can't talk to you here. I need to get out of here. You may have to swim back to shore."

"I can do that," Jennifer replied. "I won't go until we talk."

Michael put the engines in gear and pointed the bow out into the Apalachicola River and then towards the Gulf of Mexico. They would not speak again until they cleared Saint George Island and were speeding along in the open waters.

Douglas Wilson looked on in disbelief from the point at Battery Park. He had his cell phone to his ear and was saying into it, "Not only did she find The Lucy, but she found him too. She's on the boat with him right now and they are heading out into the Gulf."

He listened to the person on the other side of the phone for a moment and then replied. "Yes, I am already on it. Plenty of resources around here and I will find someone who will track them." He ended his call and continued to watch The Lucy until it had cleared Saint George Island.

Michael slowed the boat once he had lost sight of land. He turned on the auto helm and set a heading directly south and then turned to Jennifer.

"How could you do this?" He chided.

"What are you talking about?"

"Stop it, Jennifer. I saw you sitting with Douglas Wilson. I know what you are doing now."

"What, Michael? What am I doing? I didn't even know that you knew Douglas. What is going on?" She was fighting back some tears now as her anger to this line of accusations grew.

"You are working for Douglas."

"Yes, I am." She agreed.

"You are looking for me and now you found me."

"Why do you think that?"

"Because Douglas and his partner George are looking for me."

"What? Why?" Jennifer had a look of complete confusion on her face.

"Jennifer, please stop it."

"Look Michael, I work for Douglas and George. I was hired by George in Chicago to come down here and take pictures for him."

"Pictures? That's it?"

"Yes, they wanted pictures of land for sale, businesses, landscapes, and boats. Tons and tons of boats."

"That's it?" Michael was starting to listen more to what Jennifer had to say, but he was very skeptical.

"That's it. Why Michael? What's going on?"

"You first, Jennifer. You tell me how you ended up here. Then I tell you about me."

Jennifer stood up in front of Michael and said, "How about a couple of ice cold Coronas before I start?"

"Yes," Michael said. "That does sound good."

Chapter 17

George Jameson was sitting at the bar at 16 inside the Trump Tower in Chicago. He was enjoying a mixture of bourbon and a simple syrup, known as a Wooden Nickel, while he contemplated his morning. He had been in his office in the building when Douglas had called him. First to tell him that he had located The Lucy, and then later to say that he was looking at the boat heading down the river with Michael Scott on board. He knew right away that he would not be able to work anymore today. He knew that he needed a drink.

As he sat at the bar he had a wide smile on his face. He turned and looked around the spacious lobby area and restaurant and then out through the glass windows passed the city and over Lake Michigan. "Alex," he said quietly to himself. "I've finally found you Alex."

Chapter 18

"Agave, Agave, this is Saint Bernard, over." Patrick waited a minute before hailing again. "Agave, Agave, Agave, this is Saint Bernard, do you copy? Over."

Billy cherished the sound of his brother's voice on the radio. It had been four days now since he ran aground on this island and two days since he had spoken to his brother or anyone else for that matter. He had been very busy for those days moving his things off of the Lucille and making the small clearing into a front yard for his new cave home.

"Saint Bernard, this is Agave. I read you five by five."

"It's good to hear your voice Mister Sanchez. I see you on my radar now and should be there very shortly."

"Thank God, It's been very lonely here. I am ready to go home."

"Copy that, Agave. You want to give me some instructions here?"

"Copy, Saint Bernard. Come into the East bay of the island. Come in straight from the East on a two seven zero heading. The water is plenty deep and you should not have any problems getting in. Over."

"Copy, Agave. On my way." Patrick responded.

Billy was very excited about leaving this little island paradise. He had explored most of it already and had come to really enjoy its beauty and all the fruits of the trees on top of the hills. He had explored most of the caves that wandered underground through the rock with the zeal of a teenager, but he was ready to go home. He missed his wife, he missed his son who he hadn't even met yet. He desperately wanted to be with them.

"Patrick, can you hear me?" The voice cracked over the line of sight radio on Patrick's belt.

"I hear you, Billy. You doing okay?"

"I'm good. I see you coming into the bay now. Just head straight ahead to the tree line and throw me a line there. I'll tie you off to a tree."

"Can I get up to the tree line? How's the depth in here?"

"You'll be good. It has to be fifty feet or more straight down the rock wall. I haven't been able to even see the bottom there."

"Copy that. I see you now. God, it's good to lay eyes on you. Everyone back home is so worried sick about you."

"I can't wait to see them."

There was a slight pause, then Patrick said to him, "We need to talk about that, brother."

Billy was looking straight into his brother's eyes over the few feet left between them now. He felt his heart dropping and a lump form in his throat as he could see the solemn look on Patrick's face.

The brothers didn't speak much as they tied the boat snuggly to the rock ledge by using a few tall palm trees in the area to secure the lines and some rubber bumpers that Billy had brought over from the Lucille to protect his brother's boat. Once they were finished, Patrick jumped the short distance to the cleared land and took his brother in his arms. Each had tears in their eyes as they hugged and silently appreciated the moment of the uniting of two brothers who feared never seeing one another again.

"You look good." Patrick told his brother as he stepped back and looked at him.

"I feel good. I've been very busy the past few days."

"I can see that. This is a good clearing. Where's the Lucille?"

Billy pointed to the other side of the cleared trees and out to the beach beyond.

"She's out there," he said. "She's done."

"Done? What do you mean?"

"Her keel cracked, buckled the hull near the center."

"Really? Did that happen in the storm?"

"No. The next day while sitting high and dry on the beach. Come on. I'll show her to you."

They passed through to the white sand beach and Patrick was able to take in the beauty of the little cove with its sandy beach wrapping around to the tips that created the mouth of the bay to the West. Palm trees dotted the line where the sand of the beach met the palmetto bushes and there were two lone palms standing as field goals at the mouth of the bay. To his left was the sad and sobering sight of a gorgeous man made vessel that lay completely out of its element waiting for its imminent end.

"How did she get so far out of the water?" Patrick asked.

"The tide was way up due to the storm. As the water went out with the storm it left us like that."

Patrick could now see the bulging of the wood in the center of the ship and how the stern dropped dramatically from that point back at an angle to the beach below.

"That is bad," he said. "Doesn't look like she is going anywhere."

"I'm not either, am I?" Billy said quietly to his brother.

Patrick turned and looked directly into his brother's eyes.

"The Federalies have been working with the police back in Florida trying to find you. They've had your home staked out for over a week to see if you show up. You can't go home right now."

"What about Maria and the baby?"

"They are fine. The baby is healthy and the police are only after you. I'm sorry brother, but you can't go home to them right now."

"Where can I go? Should I go to Hispanola?"

"It's not safe there either. What about this little island?"

"This island? This is solitude, I'd be better off in jail."

"I can bring Maria and the baby to you." Patrick was trying to console his brother.

"Sentence my whole family to my solitude? Patrick, I can't do that."

"I know, I know. I don't know what else you can do, Billy."

Billy stopped and turned looking out to the horizon for a long moment.

"I've moved all the cargo from the Lucille," he finally said. "It's in a cave over by the clearing."

"Billy, what are you going to do?" Patrick asked him.

"Right now I'm going to get a bottle of tequila and we're going to get trashed as we watch the sun go down."

Patrick followed Billy as he went over to the opening of the large cave. It was very dark inside until Billy lit a candle and held it up revealing the large spacious room to his brother. Crates and bottles of alcohol stacked about six feet high lined the cave's walls. They had been organized by type and looked to all be intact, with the exception of a few emptied bottles left off to the side. A small cot sat in one corner where Billy had made himself a small bedroom of sorts with a table and some pictures that he had removed from his boat.

"Grab those chairs," Billy said pointing at two wooden folding chairs leaning against the cave wall. " I have the tequila and I'll grab the table."

They walked back out to the clearing and set up the table and chairs in the middle. Billy opened the tequila as Patrick climbed onto his boat and got some glasses and limes from his galley. As he came back over to the table and chairs he saw there were mangos on the table now and a few coconuts in a pile on the ground. Billy had his machete out over near a stump from a catalpa tree that he had been using to chop firewood. He took his broad knife and cut a coconut in half. At the table the brothers held up their glasses, which Patrick had poured a small amount of the alcohol into, and tapped them together.

"Here's to being alive," Billy said.

They quickly drank back the burn of the fire water and closed their eyes to hold back the tears that had started up and then setting down the glasses Patrick proclaimed, "Good stuff brother," as Billy poured more tequila.

"This one," Patrick said as he held up his glass in a toast to Billy, "is to your little tiki bar in the middle of nowhere."

"To the Nowhere Tiki Bar," Billy said.

Chapter 19

Michael was seated in the captain's chair at the helm of The Lucy. The auto helm was steering the course straight south but Michael wanted to sit in the solitary seat. He was still thoroughly upset at finding out that Jennifer was working for George and Douglas and he simply did not want to give her the ability to sit next to him at this time. He had however settled down to the point of listening now. He knew that he liked Jennifer and he wanted to hear what kind of explanation she could tell him to ease his mind about her betrayal.

Jennifer sat on a bench seat across from Michael. She was very confused about what had made Michael so upset. She desperately wanted to know what she had done wrong, but was willing to explain to him how she had come to work for George and Douglas before hearing why he was being like this.

"Michael," she started. "George Jameson originally met with me in Chicago at the Coq d'Or inside the Drake Hotel. He had originally gone by my gallery looking for me but I was at the Coq d'Or having my lunch. George was very persuasive and we needed the work so my assistant Shelby sent him over there to meet with me."

Jennifer took a drink of her beer and looked at Michael who was staring straight out in front of the boat to the horizon.

"George explained to me that he and his business partner were looking for a photographer to go down to Cedar Key and up along the shores of the Panhandle to get pictures of possible real estate investments. He told me that he needed pictures of properties, views, businesses, and boats."

"Boats?" Michael said suddenly. "Why pictures of boats for real estate investments?"

"I asked him that. He said that he wanted to see how busy the area was with boaters and tourists so he could use this information to help him decide on investing. Seemed like good reasoning to me."

Michael did not say anything but at least he was looking at her now.

She continued. "Travel photography is not normally my thing since I started my studio, but as I said earlier I needed the work. I took the job and George arranged for me to fly down to Jacksonville where I met up with Douglas. He gave me some more direction on what they were looking for and the next day I rented a car and drove to Cedar Key."

Michael sat for a few seconds thinking about what Jennifer had just told him. Searching for holes in her story. Searching for reasons to not trust her but not finding any.

Finally he asked, "Neither George or Douglas ever mentioned me?"

"No, not once."

"Did they mention anyone else?"

"No, no one. Michael, what's going on?"

"Jennifer," he said. "I believe what you are telling me but you have to understand my hesitation here. A life is at stake. Not mine, but someone that I know."

"George and Douglas are killers?"

"No, not exactly. You have to promise me that you will not tell anyone what I am going to share with you."

"Okay," she said.

Michael looked out at the horizon again. He was thinking hard about where to start and how much to tell Jennifer.

"Jennifer," he finally said. "Douglas and George are looking for me. In reality, they are looking for a friend of mine and they know that I know where he is."

Jennifer was starting directly at Michael. She didn't say a word.

"Many years ago I was an officer in the Navy. One of my best friends while I was in was a guy that I served with on board a destroyer. We were in the Persian Gulf during the first Gulf War and he and I were asked to go on a special op. We did it, and because of our actions several ships and lives were saved. We were recognized and awarded and people took notice of our performance. They immediately started recruiting us for similar work with another group within the government."

"CIA?" Jennifer asked.

"No, not CIA. It was a special group assigned to the Navy"

"Is this for real, Michael?" Jennifer was skeptical about his story.

"I turned them down," was Michael's reply. "My friend did not."

"So you're not James Bond?"

Michael smiled, "No, no. I'm double O nothing," he said.

Jennifer was happy to see him smile again.

"After my hitch with the Navy was over, I headed to Cedar Key and started bar-tending. I always enjoyed being behind the bar when I was younger and working with my father. About two years later my friend came to see me. He had been working for the government on a job and had let his feelings get in the way. He had killed a man that the government wanted dead, but he did it in a way that they could not stand behind. He was suddenly wanted by the police for murder and he was asking me to hide him."

"Who did he kill Michael? Someone that George and Douglas knew?"

"No, he killed a very bad man. A drug dealer that deserved exactly what he got."

"Then why?" She stopped.

"My friend Alex," Michael said, "is George's son."

Jennifer just looked at him. She was trying to put together the pieces. There just wasn't enough yet.

"Alex came to me in Cedar Key. He was hiding from the police. The government turned their back on him and said that there was nothing that they could do for him. I hid him on The Lucy for a few days and then I set him up with another friend of mine down in Key

West. He lived down there posing as a homeless man for a while. He wasn't truly homeless, but it allowed him to get around easily by dressing that way. Things were going very good for him then and George hadn't started searching for him yet so he could pretty much do as he wanted. Then he screwed it all up again. They called it the 'Wino Revolution.' Alex is a very smart man but he just can't leave well enough alone or just back out of any situation. He always has to go in, head on."

"What happened?" Jennifer found herself sitting forward, leaning in toward Michael.

"He got in with several of the locals and decided to try to fight the influx of rich people into The Keys. He said many of his friends were holding down three jobs just to keep up with rent and utilities. Money was coming down from New England and the Northwest and paying huge sums of money for real estate that they used two weeks out of the year. The locals couldn't afford to live there any more."

"They had a good idea and a good plan, but ultimately learned the hard way that you just can't fight city hall. Especially when their side owns city hall. The bigger problem for Alex was that someone recognized him down there and he had to come back to see me."

"Alex is in Cedar Key?" Jennifer asked.

"No," Michael replied. " He's not. He works for me now as my head bartender."

"And George is trying to find him?" Jennifer was starting to put the pieces together.

"Yeah."

"Trying to bring him to justice?"

"I'm not sure why he wants to find him. I can't take a chance though. Nobody can know where he is." Michael was looking directly at Jennifer now.

"I won't say a word Michael." She said to him.

Chapter 20

George was in a cab on his way to O'Hare International airport. His secretary had set up a flight into Pensacola for him and Douglas was currently driving there to meet up with him.

"Do you know which way they are heading?" He asked into his cell phone.

"I have a friend on the ground radar at Eglin keeping an eye on them." Douglas replied.

"Don't spook them. Michael is very smart and will be watching for anyone following him."

"I am aware. I'll keep him from knowing we're watching. I have plenty of friends to help out with that."

"Excellent. Douglas, be careful to not get too many people involved. We don't need more attention on this than we can handle."

"Understood." Douglas replied to his friend.

George ended his call with Douglas, checked his watch, and then turned to look out the side window of the cab. Chicago's Kennedy

Expressway was packed with traffic moving along steadily at seventy miles per hour. He watched as the blue line trains stopped at their scheduled stations for the loading and unloading of their patrons. He looked at his watch again. He knew that he had plenty of time to get to his flight but he definitely could not miss this plane for any reason. It had been years since he had seen or even heard from Alex. No, he could not miss this plane.

Chapter 21

Michael looked at the radar screen again. He had been monitoring it regularly since they had left Apalachicola to see if anyone seemed to be following them. He had originally set a course due south on the auto helm so that no one would know his eventual bearing and destination. After a couple of hours at trolling speeds and changing directions at random intervals he was satisfied that no one was there. Michael changed his heading and brought The Lucy up to speed. He was heading home now and he had a passenger with him.

Chapter 22

As the sun began its slow climb over the tops of the trees behind the brothers the heat was becoming unbearable on the little tropical island. The wet cold sand of the night was already dried out and the dew of the night on the leaves had already either dripped down to the foliage below or evaporated back into the air to go back through its cycle once again.

Billy was the first to stir as the beads of sweat on his forehead came together to form a stream that ran down his temple, past his earlobe and then to the back of his neck before falling to the beach below him. Immediately, the throbbing began as he attempted to open first one eye, and then the other. His mouth felt as if it had been glued shut with some sort of substance created from his saliva some sand and a large amount of salt. Slowly, he rolled over so that his hands were located beneath his chest. He then lifted himself up by pushing the earth away from him and then rolling back to his right he ended up on his butt sitting in the sand with his feet stretched out before him.

"Ouch," he said quietly, carefully.

He looked at the smoldering fire pit and then across at his brother, lying still in the sand on the other side. As his thoughts started to form again, he remembered the reality of the night before. This island was now his hideout, his jail, his home. He and Patrick had talked at great length about stripping his poor Lucille down to nothing and using her to create his house and furnishings. They would need to start today with the work because the longer they waited the more likely it was that he would change his mind and take his chances with the authorities. They would start to build a home for him on this island paradise today, but probably not until later this afternoon. He could tell that his body was insisting that a nap was soon to be in order.

Patrick woke up from his embedded imprint in the now hot sand. He was moving very slowly and hurting. Over his shoulder he noticed Billy standing in the clearing looking at the ground and then up at the tree cover above him and then out past Patricks boat to the little deep water bay. Begrudgingly he got to his feet and wandered over to his brother's side to see what he was doing.

"You're not going to forget about me out here are you?" Billy asked without looking at him.

"What? Not for a second. Why would you think that? I'll visit as much as I can. I'll bring Maria and Miguel to you. You won't be forgotten by any of us."

"I didn't think so." Billy stated almost as a matter of fact.

Patrick could see the wheels of Billy's mind spinning at nearly top speed.

"What are you thinking Billy?"

"The Nowhere Tiki Bar. I'm thinking of building a bar right here on this spot."

"A bar?"

"Yeah, I can have a marina here on the deep water side and the beach over here. It's perfect."

"If you open a bar here, the authorities will be your first customers."

"No, no, hear me out. We have friends. Some of them could use a place to get away from the same 'authorities' that are searching for me. I can make a bar for them. Just our trusted friends, that we know won't tell anyone else about it. They could help me out by bringing me supplies and I can offer them all of this."

Billy held out his hands motioning to the clearing and the island beyond it.   Patrick looked at the island with a slow sweeping eye. Thoughtfully he turned to Billy.

"That may work brother, you have the large cave that we could use for storage.   This could be a staging area for our cargos as well.   Hell, we could conduct our business right here with our friends."

"We can do this, Patrick.   The Nowhere Tiki Bar." Billy was more animated now as he turned to his brother with a big grin on his face.

"The Nowhere Tiki Bar," Patrick repeated.

The brothers began planning the bar.   A rough outline of the area where it would be, the path back to the cave, the dock for the boats to tie up.   They were   very excited about it and they jumped into their new plan with both feet.

Over the next few days they stripped all that they could from the Lucille. Leaving the electronics and engines intact so that Billy could use the radio and start the engines to charge the batteries.   Everything else was coming off.   They salvaged all the wood, metal and cloth materials as they removed them.   There was a wealth of material here and they meant to use every bit of it.

On Patrick's fifth morning on the little island he sat quietly on one of the chairs at the makeshift bar that they had set up.

"I have to go back," he said to his brother.

"I know," Billy responded from across the bar.

"I will be back in a couple weeks but I do need to get back."

"I have plenty to keep me busy for at least a few weeks. Don't worry about me."

"Okay, but I will. When I come back I'll bring more supplies and some livestock to run free on the island."

"Some pigs and chickens would be great. They're good for eating and easy to care for." Billy said.

"And lots of fresh water. We'll need to solve your water issues soon. You should be good with what I will leave from my boat until I get back."

"I'll be fine." Billy said.

The day was spent off loading supplies from Patrick's boat and making sure that Billy would be set for the time that he was to spend alone.

Missing Key

The next morning Patrick cast off his lines, gave a wave to his brother on the shore and began his trip back to Key Largo. After nearly a week with his brother at his side, Billy was all alone, again.

Chapter 23

Night had fallen across the Gulf of Mexico. Michael still had The Lucy on auto helm but he stayed up on the bridge monitoring the radar and making visual scans across the horizon. Jennifer had fallen asleep on the bench seat on the bridge that was across from him and he would steal glances at her from time to time. He was completely taken in by this woman from Chicago and really hoped that his trust in her at this moment was right. She looked so peaceful sleeping there with the moonlight shining down upon her face. She looked young and innocent like a child in her father's arms without a single concern in the world. Once Michael was completely satisfied that their course was good and that there was no ship traffic out there to be concerned about, he checked the alarms on the radar and allowed himself to take a much needed cat nap.

Chapter 24

Jennifer woke up abruptly to the screeching sound of the radar's proximity alarm going off. She could sense immediately that it was very hot out and that she had been sweating. As she tried to focus in on anything around her so that she could get her bearings, the brightness of the midmorning sun spilled into her still dilated pupils and attempted to blind her. Her senses finally started to come to her and she started to panic as she looked around the bridge, with that damn alarm going off, and realized that she did not see Michael. She stood up and stumbled around for a moment. She then looked out at the sea around her with the full expectation of seeing land or another boat that the Lucy was about to run into. Nothing was around them though. She looked out to the horizon in every direction only to find out that they were all alone. No, that she was all alone. Where was Michael?

Chapter 25

Douglas had arrived in town before George and set up rooms for both of them at the Hilton hotel down on Pensacola Beach. He then drove over to Eglin Airforce base to meet with his friend that was watching The Lucy's movements very closely. He wanted to be sure to talk to the radar operator in person and clarify the importance of keeping this as close to his chest as possible. Many lives could be at stake if the wrong group were to find out what was going on here. Afterwards Douglas returned to the hotel to meet up with George.

The two friends met the next morning down in the hotel's bar which sat right in the middle of the lobby. With its two story ceiling reaching high above the elegant space and its wide backed wooded chairs with their blue overstuffed cushions arranged for groups of four to socialize over wooden tables with games and drinks. Bloody Mary's in hand, George and Douglas sat at the Bonsai Sushi Bar and discussed how they would follow Michael. A boat, they decided, would not work very well because of the day and a half head start that Michael had on them. After discussing their different options they concluded that their only solution would be a sea plane. Douglas had many friends here in

Pensacola from his days in the military. Luckily for them this was the Home of Naval Aviation and Navy pilots were all around. Douglas knew one with just the plane they needed.

Chapter 26

Michael came up to the bridge with a pot of coffee and two cups. He could hear the alarm from below in the galley loud and clear but he had checked from the windows down there and didn't see any collision issues so he continued his business of getting the coffee. He was not prepared in any way for what he saw when he came up the ladder. Jennifer was in a total panic looking over the controls and trying to turn off the alarm. Her arms flailed about aimlessly as she reached out for buttons and then pulled back her hands before actually touching anything.

"You okay?" Michael asked from behind her.

Jennifer swung around so fast that she lost her balance and fell backwards against the throttles with her rear. The movement pushed them fully forward causing The Lucy to surge ahead and the bow of the boat to lift from the water with the extra speed. This caused Jennifer to fly back up off of the controls mostly airborne and into Michael's arms which nearly caused him to drop the fresh pot of coffee and the cups.

As he settled her back to her feet and held her until she regained her balance he asked her with a sarcastic tone in his voice. "You about finished playing around?"

"Where the hell have you been?" She yelled.

Michael carefully sat Jennifer into the captain's chair and after handing her the coffee cups, reached over to the controls and reset the speed. He turned off the alarm and checked the radar before looking at their heading and resetting the auto helm. Turning back to Jennifer, he reached back for the cups and holding up the pot in his hand said to her, "Coffee?"

Jennifer glared at him for a moment and allowed her heart rate to come down some.

"Yes, thank you," she replied with what Michael determined to be a little overtone of anger.

Jennifer stood up with her cup and moved back over to the bench seat and quietly tried to enjoyed her morning coffee. Michael explained to her that the alarm had probably picked up some sea clutter or a whale or something. He apologized for not responding to the alarm quicker so that she wouldn't have panicked, but that he was accustomed to these alarms going off from time to time and referred to it as "life at sea." After a while Jennifer settled back down as the two of them started to talk again as they had on that first night on the balcony in Cedar Key. The sun was getting hotter now and she told Michael that she would like to tan again. She went down to the stateroom where her clothes were still in her bags and took out her bikini. After washing up she looked at her bikini for a moment and smiled as a completely devilish idea came to her mind. She had wanted Michael from the first time that she had seen him. The days and nights that they had spent together so far had not afforded them that opportunity. She was going to create that opportunity now.

Chapter 27

Alex Jameson sat in an adirondack chair on the beautiful and secluded white sand beach of the West bay of Missing Key. With his cup of coffee, a bottle of Tylenol, and a Bloody Mary all within reach he stared out over the aqua blue water of the bay. The light waves of the late morning ran up the beach to innocently touch his toes and then quickly returned to the bay before making another sneak attack on his bare feet.

Sitting there with his eyes mostly closed behind his Ray Ban sunglasses Alex was trying to remember the events of the previous night while at the same time figuring out what fruits and vegetables he would need for the upcoming evenings festivities.

"I'm thinking mango and coconut," he said aloud to his two compadres.

Ollie just sat there quietly and turned an ear to Alex. He really had no suggestions for the days menu and besides, he was completely mesmerized by the sight of his best friend in the world Stanley as he ran around on the beach chasing sandpipers. The little birds would scurry about quickly until they would tire of sprinting with their tiny legs and break into flight. Stanley would then follow them out into the clear salt water until he was deep enough that it would splash up to his chest and the errant spray would go into his mouth and give him that salty taste that could choke a horse. He loved the salt water and the way that his golden brown hair felt when it had a good coat of salt on it. Stanley was a mutt, a complete and total mutt.

Ollie, on the other hand, was very loyal and loved to be seated at Alex's side. From there he would watch Stanley run around like the totally free animal that he was. Ollie always listened attentively to Alex's every word and then, as if he had contemplated every thought that had been put to him, he would completely agree.

Alex patted his good friend on the top of his head. The black lab turned to him briefly with a what seemed to be a smile and then turned his attention back to Stanley.

"Stanley is having himself a good time this morning," he said.

"May even catch one of those sandpipers today. I've always wondered what he might do if he ever manages to catch one."

Alex and Ollie sat and watched the show for a while longer. Stanley was most definitely the best performer on the island. He had never put on a bad show and didn't care about receiving any recognition for his performance. All he needed was a scratch under the chin and a good belly rub from time to time.

After finishing his Bloody Mary, Alex stood up.

"Time to get the day started," he said. "The pirates get restless if the rum is not ready to be poured."

Chapter 28

Jennifer was laying out on the back of The Lucy soaking in the gulf sun for all it was worth. She couldn't help but smile from ear to ear, like a little child who had just been given a new toy that had been their most wanted item in the world, when she heard Michael coming down the stairs. She felt all the hairs on her body stand on end as a chill that started in her feet worked its way up her legs and spine until it ended at the base of her skull where her nerves connected to her restless brain.

Get control of yourself she thought. Relax and let the moment happen.

Michael came down the steps from the cockpit into the aft section of the boat. He had been in the heat of the sun for a while now and needed to get himself an ice cold beer. He glanced up to where he knew Jennifer was lying in the sunlight to get a quick glimpse of her. Stopping with the loud thud of his feet on the teak flooring, he struggled as his mind tried to comprehend that he was seeing Jennifer there before him, naked to all the world. Her darkly tanned skin shimmered in the sunlight with a glistening of sweat that was visible from her shoulders down along her entire back and buttocks and then down her thighs to her calves. She was radiant and beautiful and Michael was unable to move as he stood behind her and quietly stared.

Jennifer could feel his eyes on her. She could feel the heat from his stare that made the noontime sun feel like an ice cold mountain stream running over all of her at once. She wanted to turn towards Michael to look him in the eye and invite him over to her. She did not. Instead she laid there perfectly still and allowed him to consume the vision before him. A naked woman who had not openly invited him but had instead sent out an ambiguous invitation that he would need to translate. Yes, she thought as she silently lay there, leave the next move to him. Her chest filled with excitement as she stifled a smile and a little laugh. Please don't take too long, my dear.

As Michael began to regain his ability to think and move, he slowly moved towards Jennifer. His eyes were taking in all of her with one long look. Her thick brown hair rolling off her shoulders and that skin, that dark tanned skin with the short blonde hair standing out in contrast. Michael walked over to her, instinctively, and gently set his hand down in the small of her back. Jennifer let out a quiet moan of acceptance that let Michael know that this was okay. He lifted his palm leaving his fingertips in contact with her body and slowly slid them first up to the middle of her back and then changing course he moved back across the small of her back and up over the soft firm cheek of her buttocks and again lowered his palm as he reached her thigh. Gently he squeezed the back of her thigh in his hand and started his way back up to her rear. As he approached, Jennifer instinctively arched her back lifting her ass slightly as Michael took one whole cheek in his hand and firmly caressed it. He was ready and Jennifer could sense it. She, too was ready and nearly about to explode with the excitement that had been building up inside her. She wanted him badly and she wanted him right there and now.

Rolling away from Michael, Jennifer had turned over and was now able to look directly up at him. She had exposed her naked breasts to him as he sat next to her in the place in the couch that she had just vacated. Michael had slid his hand from her bottom as she had rolled and was now resting it on her slim waist line. He again looked at her naked body and lustfully looked at her flat stomach. He could feel the muscle of it now below his thumb as he slid his hand back until he could feel her protruding hip bone under the palm of his hand. He squeezed again and took a deep breath as he closed his eyes with anticipation. When he opened them again, he looked into Jennifer's eyes and slowly leaned forward to her. He took his hand from her hip and reached down carefully taking her head into his hands and kissed her deeply.

Chapter 29

Stanley raced up the brush covered trail far ahead of Alex and Ollie. This was a daily trip for the trio and he was always excited to be the first to the top of the hill. As he ran he was sure to stop around the high weeds that covered the large holes that lead far down into the caves below. He knew where each of the holes were located and was careful not to get too close as he inspected each one. When he reached the top of the climb he turned around to watch and wait for his two companions. He knew that they would not be very far behind.

Alex and Ollie came into sight from around the last bend before the top. Alex was carrying his mesh diver's bag over his shoulder with a few coconuts in it that he had found along the way. Stanley let out a small yelp in an attempt to tell the two laggers to hurry up. He had been waiting for what seemed to him to be a life time and he wanted to get to the vegetable gardens and even more importantly, the caves. The vegetable gardens were not of much interest to him since he was no longer allowed in there after the spoiled dill incident. Ever since that bad batch of pickles Alex had put up a fence and banned the dogs from the garden. Now he was interested in the caves. He wanted to chase the bats in circles as he scared them from their perch inside. Then he would end up running away from them as their circle tightened to a frenzy as they sounded their radars off of trees and rocks to find their way.

As Alex and Ollie reached the top of the hill, Stanley raced off for the cave. Alex stopped and began hunting around the trees for some fresh mango. Once he found a few ripe enough, he cut them down with his machete and placed them in the bag. He found a few more coconuts lying on the ground and when he felt like he had enough of the fruits headed down to the vegetable garden for some peppers, tomatoes, and herbs for that night's dinner and drinks at the bar.

Back on the trail on his way down to the caves, Alex stopped suddenly when he noticed Ollie standing frozen and looking straight ahead of them. Ollie's fur was standing on end at the top of his head between his ears as well as on his back between his shoulder blades and a small patch above his tail.

Alex whispered to him, "Quiet boy," as he squatted down by his friend and looked ahead to see what had attracted all of his attention. Slowly and carefully Alex reached his right hand back over his shoulder and took his machete from its sheath which was attached to his back pack. Bringing the knife down slowly in front of him, he kept his eyes out to the front studying the shrubs to both sides of the trail. The faint crack of a small brittle tree branch being stepped on was heard and Ollie could not stifle his growl. Alex rested his left hand on Ollie's back and quietly said to him, "This little piggy went wee, wee, wee all the way home." Then he yelled, "Go get him boy!"

Ollie ran off down the trail at full speed. As he closed in on the spot where they had heard the noise there was suddenly a flurry of movement in the bushes as Ollie dove in barking as angrily as he could. Alex was running down the trail towards all the commotion in the bushes. He could not see anything but moving leaves and branches when suddenly a wild pig came running out onto the trail and almost hit Alex's legs before changing course and running up the trail towards the top of the hill. Alex had spun around as the pig moved about this feet and all but fell over trying to not be run over by it. Ollie then came jumping out of the shrubs but he was not able to change course in time and ran right into Alex's legs causing both of them to fall to the ground. Ollie stood back up and looked at Alex, not sure what had just taken place. He then looked up the trail for the pig and then back at Alex. Alex was sitting on the trail with both legs out in front of him looking at Ollie and laughing.

"Guess that one outsmarted us both," he said. "We'll have our revenge another day and serve him up with barbecue sauce."

Ollie walked over and put his cold nose to Alex's leg.

"I know, back to work." Alex said as he got back to his feet and they started toward the caves once again.

Chapter 30

Michael sat on the couch on the stern of The Lucy totally naked. He had his head leaning on the back of the couch as he stared up at the blue sky above. Jennifer was laying on the couch with her head on his thigh also staring up.

"That was great," she said to him. "Thank you for that."

"Oh no," he replied. "Thank you."

They both let out a little laugh.

"Michael?" Jennifer asked, "Where exactly are we going?"

Michael thought for a moment.

"Us?" he finally asked, "Or the boat?"

Jennifer smiled. She hadn't thought about the double meaning of the question before she had asked it.

"The boat," she said. " We have been going for over a day now and you haven't said where we are headed."

"I'm sorry. I should have said something to you earlier. I'm taking you to my home."

"Your home?"

"Well, my island, where I live on The Lucy and run a dive of a bar."

"Your island?" Jennifer was a bit skeptical.

"No one else has claimed it and the bar on it was given to me. So yes, I would say that it is my island."

Jennifer was looking up at him and he was gazing down into her eyes. They sat for a while studying each other.

Michael finally broke the silence.

"I need to go and check on our course and the radar," he said.

Jennifer reluctantly lifted her head and let Michael stand up. She then turned on her side as she watched him grab the towel that she had brought out to lay on and wrapped it around his waist. He climbed the stairs to the open cockpit above and once out of sight she rolled onto her back and smiled.

Chapter 31

Alex and Ollie reached the vegetable garden at the foot of the trail. Stanley was over in the cave barking and then running from his own echo. The bats were stirring from all the noise and were starting to make their little bombing runs by swooping down on Stanley. Ollie looked over at the commotion and seemingly shook his head as he turned his attention back to Alex.

"Everything is looking good Ollie," Alex said. " Looks like we may want to fertilize today though. The dirt is starting to look a little dry."

Ollie started to wag his tail and stood up with excitement. Not really from any desire to fertilize, but because he heard his name mentioned.

"Stanley!" Alex suddenly yelled, "Come on out here and stop messing with the bats. I need to gather some dung and I don't need them all pissed off."

After gathering some peppers and vegetables for the day and adding them to his dive bag with the fruit he had already gathered, Alex grabbed the shovel that was leaning against the fence surrounding the garden and headed to the cave. He scooped some bat dung off of the cave floor and took it out to the garden and spread it around. Stanley and Ollie were down by the beach playing with some crabs that were scurrying about. Alex took a piece of the feces and threw it, hitting Stanley squarely in the back of the head. Startled, he spun around to see what hit him and then shook his head wildly. Looking down at the dung, he sniffed it and snorted as he recognized the scent. He then took off like a flash into the surf and jumped around in the salt water trying to clean his coat. Ollie walked up to the edge of the water getting only his front paws wet and watched the show.

Chapter 32

Michael sat at the helm of The Lucy. He had checked his position on the GPS and was monitoring the radar as well as the horizon. Jennifer came up behind him still naked and carrying two Coronas.

"Cervezas?" She asked while handing out one of the beers.

"Gracias," Michael replied as he turned to take the glistening bottle from her. He stopped in motion once again as he saw her standing there. Her tan firm breasts, with the hot midday sun beating down on them, and her flat abs showing a rippling hint of muscle. She stood before him almost as a vision. Naked in the open air as if God himself had just created her minutes ago. He slowly took his beer from her without once looking away. She brought gifts as well, he thought. She is an angel.

Jennifer smiled at Michael as she watched him checking her out.

"How we looking, Captain?"

"Umm, well....what?" was the only response that he had.

"Our course? Are we getting close to your home?"

"Oh, yes. It's just now coming onto the radar," Michael turned away from Jennifer and pointed to the radar screen.

"Right there," he said.

Jennifer stepped in closer to Michael letting the bare skin of her breast touch his   shoulder as she leaned in to see what he was pointing at.

"That looks like a giant spider," she said to him.

"I know," he replied. "It's an amazing little island that everyone seems to overlook. That's the best part of it."

"Is that where your bar is?"

"Yep. Right there in the middle of the island. It looks out over both of these bays. The bay to the West is a beautiful white sand beach with coral reefs out about one hundred feet from shore. Great for snorkeling and the sunset is gorgeous."

"Sounds amazing," she said.

"It really is. This bay to the East," he said pointing at the islands image on the radar screen, "is about a mile deep right up to the shore."

"Really? That's crazy."

"A meteor hit the earth here millions of years ago and made the deep hole and forced the sea bed up creating the island the way that it is. It is really a great place for a bar."

"I can't wait to see it," Jennifer said. "How long until we get there?"

"Should be there in about an hour," he said.

"Very good," she replied. Reaching down she opened the towel that was covering Michael and proclaimed, "Then we have a little time."

Chapter 33

George sat in the front seat of the Dehavilland float plane looking out his right side window to the sea below. Douglas was in the row behind him sitting on the left side of the plane.

"How long until we see them?" George asked Douglas and the pilot.

"Should be another hour or more according to the radar tracks from the operators at Eglin," the pilot said.

"They tracked them on a straight course out of Apalachicola. After a few east and west tacks where they were probably trying to see if they were being followed, they seemed to follow a straight course towards Mexico."

"Well, thank your military brothers for tracking them so well and not being seen. With a little luck I will have my son back before this day is out."

"Copy that, sir. Glad that we could help you out."

The pilot went back to checking his instruments and radioed back to the radar operators for more directions. This was good exercise for them and a very welcome distraction from the normal monotony of training and observing.

Douglas turned on his switch to the microphone in his headset and asked George, "What is your plan if we find Alex?"

"I'm not sure I have a plan," George responded. "Just want to find him first."

Douglas sat back in his seat and watched the sea pass below the plane. He was really hoping that they would find Alex when they finally caught up to Michael.

Chapter 34

Alex and the two dogs arrived back at the bar to find Raphael and Sonia, the couple from the sailboat "Galileo," sitting at one of the bar tables going over a chart. They had sailed out of Italy nearly three months ago and were charting out their course through the Caribbean and Gulf waters before eventually heading back to their Mediterranean home. A friend of theirs from the Dominican Republic had told them about Missing Cay years before and had sworn them to secrecy before giving them the location. This was not their first trip to this little island. They had been here on previous trips to the Americas and Mexico and were considered locals here now.

"Ciao, Raphael, Sonia," Alex said as he came into the bar. "Come stai?"

"Bene, Alex," replied Raphael. "And how are you and your two friends today?" He continued.

"Doing good, thanks. Just picked up some fruits and vegetables for this evening. You two going to stick around for dinner?"

"Yes, Alex. We'll be here until tomorrow at least. Planning on going into Havana for a few days once we leave here but Sonia wants to see another sunset here before we go."

"Great plan you guys. Dinner will be chicken on the grill with whatever fresh fish or seafood the guys on the *Shark Fin* bring back. Almost had us some pork to roast on the grill, but he got past Ollie and all but ran me over to make his escape."

"We have some olives and smoked salmon that we can add to the meal as appetizers if you wish." Sonia offered.

"That would be great. Dinner will be a few hours yet. Are you ready for some drinks?"

"You know we are my friend. How about something with a little rum in it?"

"I'm on it," Alex replied. "I have some fresh coconut here too. I'll make you something special."

Chapter 35

Jennifer was standing next to Michael as he took The Lucy safely into the East Harbor of Missing Cay. Wearing her Victoria Secret bikini top and a pair of khaki linen shorts, she looked ahead at the canopy of trees that covered nearly the entire island. There was a large sailboat tied up very close to land and the mast seemed to be camouflaged right into the trees. From the center of the island which seemed to be right at sea level the tree tops rose to the North and the South creating what appeared to be a valley. There were steep cliffs of rock on both sides of the bay that dropped straight down into the shimmering water below.

She took in the landscape with her eyes wide open and turned her head sharply to the right when she thought that she had heard the faint barking of dogs on the shore. After a moment of concentrating on the land she saw them. Two dogs running, jumping, and barking along the top of the cliff to the North.

"That's Stanley and Ollie," Michael said. "You'll meet them in a minute."

As they moved closer to the valley center she began to see a cave or hole in the trees that seemed to be opening up. It was very near where the sailboat was and there appeared to be movement inside.

"That's my bar," Michael told her.

"What is?" She asked. "That cave?"

"That's no cave." Michael said. "That's the best hidden secret in all the sea. That is The Nowhere Tiki Bar."

"Hidden? How do you make money form a bar that nobody knows about?" She asked.

"Locals only." He claimed, "Been like that since 1968."

"Locals? Are you nuts? The only locals her are two dogs, some fish, and those pelicans."

Michael smiled, "Yeah, but the pelicans drink lots and tip very well."

Jennifer just looked at him.

As they closed in on the cave Jennifer noticed now that she could see straight through to the other side of the island. She remembered the image on the radar screen and then looked harder until she could make out the white sand beach on the other side. She then saw that there were people standing in the cave as well. It looked like two men and a woman. They were at the edge of the water looking their way and waving. She instinctively waved back.

Chapter 36

Michael slowed the boat until it had almost stopped, he turned the wheel and let his floating home turn and drift slowly until it lightly bumped the dock. He had carefully docked The Lucy in behind the sailboat and in front of another boat that Jennifer had not seen until they had just barely missed it when maneuvering in.

Jennifer watched as one of the men jumped onto the back of the boat and tied a line to one of the cleats. She saw Michael, who had moved to the front of the boat, catch a line from the other man and tie it off. They had arrived. They were in Missing Key.

As Michael returned to where Jennifer was standing, she turned and was surprised to see that the man that had jumped on the back of the boat was standing right beside her.

"Hola," he said to her. "I'm Alex."

"Alex?" Jennifer responded and after a moment for her thoughts to catch up, "Oh! You're Alex."

Alex looked at her with a bit of surprise.

"So, you know who I am?" He asked. Then with a glance over at Michael, he said, "And how is it that I don't know you?"

Michael stepped in.

"Alex, this is Jennifer. We met in Cedar Key and have been traveling together for the past few days. Jennifer, this is Alex. Please excuse his rudeness. He's been on this island a little too long."

"Rudeness?" Alex countered, "Just being hospitable to our guest. You didn't radio ahead and let me know to expect guests."

"I couldn't radio," Michael said as he looked directly at his friend. "Help me get The Lucy secured and offload the supplies. Then we need to talk."

Alex looked back at Michael and understood right away that there was some urgency in his statement. They had been through a lot over the years and could read each other as if they were brothers.

As Michael and Alex secured The Lucy with the help of Raphael and Sonia, Jennifer went down below to do a little prep work with her makeup. Two full days on the open sea had taken a little toll on her skin and she wanted to freshen up. Once finished she came up to see that the others were all standing together at what appeared to be the bar. She went ashore and walked across the planks of heavy wood that made up the floor to meet with them.

Standing with the group now, Jennifer was formally introduced to Raphael and Sonia. Michael explained that they had come over to the Caribbean on their sailboat from Marina di Camerota in Italy. He explained that this was not their first trip here and how they had become locals at the bar when they were introduced to it by a dear friend of The Nowhere Tiki Bar from the Dominican Republic.

Michael handed Jennifer a Corona and told her that he would show her around the island some. She had already noticed the wood floor that she had crossed over and was now standing on with the others. The planks were a little wider than she was used to seeing and the finish looked like a worn paint job. The bar that they had been standing at was teak and had many various carvings in it from patrons that had come here before her. What few walls there were, had black and white photos of men and their families swimming in the waters of the sea and fishing from their trawlers. There were hundreds of brass nautical fixtures hanging about as if in memorial to a long lost ship that was being honored here. As they crossed outside to the beach on the western bay she was amazed by the beauty and contrast of this side of the island. Just a few steps from where the boat was docked in mile deep water they were staring out at an aqua blue hidden treasure.

There were palm trees growing up from the sand, casting long shadows down onto the beach as they reached out over the water before turning up towards the sky. Immediately Jennifer headed to the edge of the water where she kicked off her flip flops and walked in ankle deep. She then looked back at Michael.

"This is gorgeous, Michael. I can't believe this place exists and the whole world doesn't know about anything about it."

Michael looked at her, "And they can't know. You do realize that?"

"Yes, I do. I was just commenting on the beauty here."

As Michael and Jennifer were standing in the water and talking a sea plane flew directly overhead at tree level nearly forcing both of them to their knees in the translucent water. Michael watched as the plane soared back to the heavens and banked hard to the left as the pilot searched for a place in the harbor to safely land. Michael quickly turned and ran up to the tiki bar and left Jennifer standing alone watching as the plane made its mesmerizing maneuvers. Not sure what she should do, she finally decided to follow Michael up the beach.

Inside the bar Michael, Raphael, and Sonia were all standing together talking in a very hurried manner. Jennifer joined up with them and gave Michael a puzzled look.

"It's George," he said.

"George? How did he find us?"

"Yes, George. I don't know how he followed us, but we don't know where Alex is. Do you understand?"

"Where could he have gone?" she asked.

"No, listen to me, Jennifer. We do not know where he is. Do you understand?" Michael explained slowly.

"Got it," she replied as the realization of what Michael was saying to her sank in.

The float plane came right up to the beach before the pilot shut down the engines and brought the propeller to a stop. George stepped out of the seaplane door and down onto the pontoon before stepping off of that and into the sand. His Sperry Topsider deck shoes left flat footsteps behind him as he continued up the beach to where the tiki bar was hidden in the trees. George was dressed in a pair of khaki cargo shorts and a white polo style shirt with a Nautica emblem on the left breast. His aviator sunglasses finished off an ensemble that was completely nautical and made him look like he could possibly be a local here at Missing Key.

Douglas, on the other hand, while looking rather dapper in his white southern gentlemen suit, did not fit in quite so well as he followed George through the sand. Both of the men walked under the canopy and into the Nowhere Tiki Bar where the group stood looking back at them. George looked around the bar taking in all of the comfortable and almost familiar looking surroundings that had been created here.

"George!" Jennifer said aloud, "What are you doing here?"

George looked at Jennifer and without responding to her he looked at Michael and said very adamantly, "Where is Alex?"

Michael looked directly back at him without blinking and stated, "He's not here, George."

"No? I find that hard to believe," he retorted.

"Look around," Michael said to him, "do you see him?"

"Not yet, Michael but, I know that you are hiding him somewhere.

"Why are you looking for him, George? Why can't you just let him be?"

"He's my son. He's a fugitive from the law and he is my son which makes him my responsibility."

"He's a grown man. He is very capable of taking care of himself and he is his own responsibility." Michael snapped back.

"Look Michael, I am here to find Alex and take him back with me. Please just make this easier on both of us and tell me where he is."

"He is not here, George."

"Look," George said again. "This is a quiet little sanctuary you have here. Not too many people even know about it do they? Sure would be a shame if I had to bring the U.S. Navy and Marine Corp down here to search the island for him. That just might do a little harm to your anonymity here."

Michael stood there looking at him. His anger was beginning to grow from the threat that had just been made to him.

"Why?" Jennifer asked. "Why would you do that? Why can't you just let Alex be? You know the government has deserted him and just left him to fend for himself on this."

"What do you know?" George barked at her.

"I know you lied to me and used me in an effort to find someone that doesn't need to be found." Jennifer said as her anger too, started to grow.

"You know nothing," he said to her in a more composed voice now. "Nor do you Michael. I need to find my son. I can help him."

"Help him?" Michael sounded a bit surprised. "How can you help him? You know that he doesn't deserve to go to jail."

"I know that and I need to talk to him and take him home. Please just help me help him. I don't have much choice here and I hate to threaten you, but you know that I can have the military here in under an hour if I need to. This is that important to me."

Michael looked at George for a long moment and then said, "I cannot tell you where Alex is, George. I'm sorry."

"Then so am I." George said.

Alex suddenly emerged from a hidden cave entrance that was located behind the bar. He looked at George and Douglas and said, "Don't do it dad."

"Alex," George said. "Son, you look good. I've been worried sick about you."

"I know dad. I couldn't contact you though. They turned their backs on me. They sent me out to do something for them and then turned their backs at the first sign of problems."

"I know they did son."

"I can't go back. I can't go to jail for them."

"I can help you, Alex. I've talked to people that can help you."

"Who, dad?" Alex asked urgently, "Who did you talk to?"

"Senator Shelton."

"Senator Shelton? Oh my God, no. Dad, he was the man in charge of my unit. He's the one that pulled all of my support and turned his back when it started to become politically dangerous for him."

"What? But, he said he would help."

"Dad, he's using you to find me. As long as I am running free I am a threat to him."

"Oh my God."

"Dad, how did you find me?"

"I sent Jennifer to find Michael. She had no idea what I was doing but I had heard that he was in Cedar Key and came up with a plan to try to find him using her. I never imagined that she would end up traveling here with him, I just wanted pictures of him or The Lucy. When they both showed up in Apalachicola, Douglas and I stepped into high gear to follow them here."

"Follow us?" Michael asked, "How did you do that? I checked radars and was very careful with setting my course."

"Military radar from Eglin," George said. "Douglas has friends on the base there."

"Military? Dad, you've led them to me."

"What? No, these are friends of Douglas's and we kept it to just the fewest people that we needed involved."

Alex looked over at Michael. "They're coming. I'm sorry about Missing Key. I'm sorry that I got you involved in any of this."

Michael looked back at him, "Don't worry about any of that. What can we do to help?"

"I have to go. Help me get my boat set."

"They'll follow you, Alex. They already have a radar on us."

"No, I have to get out of here and lead them away from Missing Key. Help me Michael, please."

George looked at Alex, "I'm sorry, son. I only wanted to help you."

"I know, dad. It's okay, I'll be okay."

Michael and Alex ran over to Alex's Chris-Craft. Jumping onto the boat Alex quickly started the engines while Michael ran over to the lines and casting them off of the cleats, he threw them onto the boats deck.

"Be safe, Alex. You know how to find me later."

"Yes, I know. Thank you."

Alex went below to the lower cabin to steer the boat. This would keep anyone from being able to see him on the deck by using satellite imagery. He pointed the boat to the mouth of the harbor and immediately set it up on a plane as he put the throttles to the full forward position. After clearing the harbor the boat changed course towards the Yucatan Straights and quickly headed out to the horizon.

Michael had already turned back to the group in the Nowhere Tiki Bar. Before the boat had made it out of the harbor he was yelling to George and Douglas that they needed to get off the island before anyone showed up.

"George, Douglas, you guys need to go now. If you care at all about Alex you'll leave now and head back home."

"But," George started. "Is Alex going to be okay?"

"He will be fine but you need to go now. Don't try to follow him either. They're tracking you. When you get back just tell them that you found us anchored out on a secluded cay fishing and skinny dipping."

"I'll do that," he said. "I'm sorry. I just want Alex to be okay. Douglas, come on. We need to go."

George and Douglas ran back to the plane where their pilot was sitting on the pontoon with his feet in the water.

"What was all that noise?", the pilot asked.

"We spooked some guy and his girlfriend skinny dipping. He got all mad at us and took off in his boat."

George helped the pilot and Douglas push the plane back into deeper water where they spun around and took off towards the western opening of the bay and then turned to the North as they headed back to Pensacola. George didn't even look towards the horizon in the direction that the boat had gone. He felt very bad now that he had uprooted Alex again and forced him to have to find a new safe place to live. I was only trying to help you son, was all that he could think.

Three days later George was sitting in his apartment in the John Hancock building in Chicago watching an all news channel when the story came across.

"A boat believed to be owned by wanted fugitive, Alex Jameson, was found floating one hundred miles off the coast of Honduras today." The news reporter said. "It had run out of fuel and was found adrift at sea. No one was found on board the vessel and the U.S. Navy and Coast Guard have conducted a thorough search for survivors in the area. At this point, no one has been found."

George turned off the television.

"Alex," he whispered aloud. "I hope that you are okay. I am so sorry for chasing after you."

The voice from behind startled him completely.

"I'm fine dad. I do need your help now."

Chapter 37

Nearly three weeks had passed when Billy heard the welcome sound on the line of sight radio.

"Missing Key, Missing Key, this is the beer truck. Do you copy?"

"Beer Truck, this is Missing Key, you are a sight for sore eyes. Your line is straight. I can't wait to see you."

"Copy that, Missing Key. Many new flavors for you."

Billy sat the radio down on the bar top and watched as Patrick maneuvered his boat through the natural channel into the bay and that was when he first saw her. Maria was a striking beauty at five foot six inches tall. Her dark brown hair falling down over her bare tanned shoulders and revealing the thin almost fragile collar bone of a woman that weighed all of one hundred and five pounds. Maria was anything but fragile, though. She was stunning and strong. Her upbringing in Hispanola by a stringent father and a doting mother created a well rounded, disciplined and independent mind within a beautiful and strong body. She was completely irresistible to all men and completely devoted to her one and only true love, Billy.

She stood on the bow of the boat staring straight ahead at Billy, knowing that she would start crying at the sight of him. She fulfilled this prophecy completely as the tears started to cloud her vision. He had changed in his appearance. Thinner and leaner and as darkly tanned as a Scottish man could get, he looked healthy to her as they closed in. Healthy and happy and crying.

As Patrick closed in on the shoreline and maneuvered the boat sideways, Maria leaped to the shore and ran into Billy's arms, leaving Patrick to his own adeptness to tie up the boat up to the dock.

"I've missed you," Maria said. "I have worried so much about you every moment of every day since you've been gone."

"I'm sorry, my Maria. I am so sorry."

She looked into his eyes and took in all of the lines and ridges of his face. He had clearly not shaven in nearly a week and the grey whiskers of his chin seemed to shimmer in the sunlight.

"You have no reason to be sorry.", she said to him.

"I did not keep my promise. I didn't make it back for my son's birth. I needed to be there for you. For both of you."

"You did all that you could, my love. You stayed alive for us."

"I am still very sorry for what I have put you through, my Maria."

They embraced again and then slowly took notice of Patrick who was sitting on the edge of his boat looking at all that Billy had accomplished while he was gone. Maria turned to see what Patrick was looking at and while she did not walk away from Billy, she turned her head from him and took in all of his hard work.

"You did all this?" She asked.

"Had to keep the hands busy in an attempt to keep the mind occupied."

"It's amazing, Billy. You're amazing.", she said.

The three of them looked at the bar that Billy had created. The floor had been made of the hull planks of the Lucille. Beneath that he had used the rigid boards of the ship's keel and frame to create a joist system mounted to the rock of the island. The bar was made of the teak wood that had been used in the pilot house and staterooms onboard the boat. It was a beautiful place that was completely open to the island's deep east bay to one side, with its steep cliffs leading down to the dark blue waters below. Then there was the west bay, with its white sand beach and palms that surrounded the green waters that could only be found in the tropics.

Maria slowly turned now and walked away from Billy leaving a hand in his as he followed her out to the beach.

"Billy, this is absolutely gorgeous. I am finding myself jealous of you now."

"Don't be. It has only just now become gorgeous with you standing there in the middle of it all."

Maria looked into his deep blue eyes and smiled at him with all the love that she could muster from deep inside her heart. Billy wanted to just stand there and be close to his wife. It had been months since they had seen each other and so much had happened to both of them in that time. He wanted to just stay there with her and hold her in his arms but he knew that there was work to get done first. Taking her hand, he led her back under the buttonwood canopy and over to Patrick's boat. There they started to unload all types of supplies.

The chickens and wild pigs were the first to come off. Patrick had complained the whole way about the terrible smell that they made. He had yelled at them several times that he was ready to make that night's menu items out of them if they didn't disappear out of his sight into the island quickly. There were bags of feed for the animals, although they would have plenty to choose from with all that the island naturally supplied. Patrick had also brought some seeds so that Billy could start a garden, and shovels and pick axes so that they could get to work on a cistern so there would be enough fresh drinking water. An extra water tank had been installed by Patrick on his boat so that with each trip out he could bring extra fresh water with him. The brothers were off to a very good start of making this lost little treasure of an island into a home and a meeting place for the people that they knew best.

Chapter 38

"Alex." George said. "Son, you're okay. Thank god."

"I'm fine dad." Alex replied.

"How did you get away from them? Where did you go?"

"I never left the island. As my boat was speeding out of the harbor I slid over the side and swam to the shore. Michael and I had worked out an escape plan years ago. It's always a good thing to have a plan."

"Alex," George looked at his son. "What happened? Why are they doing this to you?"

"Dad." Alex paused and walked over to the window overlooking the distant lights of Chicago. "When I got out of the Navy, the government taught me to be a killer."

"A killer? What do you mean?"

"I was an assassin, dad. I killed bad people for the government."

George sat silently as Alex explained the years after he left the Navy. He was very surprised by what he heard. He could not imagine that his son had lived such a life as this.

When Alex paused from the revelation George spoke up in a calm voice.

"Son," he said. "If they trained you for all of this and sent you on the missions, why are they after you?"

Alex looked at his father, "The last mission that I was on went very badly. Senator Shelton was my commanding officer. He wasn't a senator at the time but a captain in the Navy. He had served as a SEAL for years before the government asked him to start up and run the team that I was on. It was his pet project. We were tasked with taking out the drug cartels, that threatened the United States, from the tops of their organizations. We had a hit list of drug lords throughout the Caribbean and Latin American countries and we were going to get them all."

"This was government sanctioned?" George asked.

"It was a very specific duty that we had. Shelton was on a war path to get all of them."

"It doesn't sound legal, Alex."

"It's not, but since when does the government ever care about what's legal when we are doing the 'good of the people.'?"

George didn't respond to his son. They both understood that what was going on wasn't right but it didn't matter now.

"What about the last mission?" George finally asked.

"It started out in New Orleans." Alex said. "I was on a vacation there when I stumbled upon Jean Hinault, the head of a small drug cartel out of Haiti. We hadn't stepped him up on our hit list yet, but since I had happened upon him purely by accident, I had to seize the opportunity. I was in the French Quarter, with my girlfriend at the time Kate, when I saw Jean at the Sazerac Bar inside The Roosevelt Hotel. I immediately ended my vacation and went into high gear of scoping out the area and setting up a plan. I sent Kate back to Jacksonville and started following Jean everywhere he went to establish a plan that would help me reach my objective. I notified the Team and got the formal approval to go ahead with my ideas. With as much research as I could do, I was able to find out from the hotel, that he would be staying there for a week and observed that he would normally set his dinner reservations for around 8pm each night. I decided that a sniper shot at the entrance of The Roosevelt from a rooftop two blocks away on Baronne Street would be my best chance. I could take a shot as he came out of onto the sidewalk before he got into his car to go to dinner. With my plan all set I notified the Team and they dispatched a man to bring me the guns and supplies that I would need."

George sat quietly listening to every word that Alex told him. He could hardly believe what he was hearing but did not want to interrupt his son.

"I had set the day," Alex went on. "Everything was in place. I made my way up to my perch and readied my gun and scope. I sat quietly as the time approached and concentrated on the shot. I went over my escape route in my head several times and was very comfortable because I knew that I had already practiced it several times as well. I sat there on that roof top with my eye to my rifle's scope and waited patiently. That was when everything went wrong."

Alex paused for a moment as a tear formed in his eye and a lump started in his throat. He was looking out over the city skyline of Chicago as he remembered that day.

George sat quietly and watched his son put the words together in his head. Finally, Alex began to speak again.

"As Jean's bodyguards stepped out of the hotel onto the street I could feel my excitement rise as my adrenaline built. With my finger resting on the trigger, I moved the scope from face to face looking closely at each of them for the one that I wanted. That's when I saw her walk out. Kate's face suddenly filled my scope and I went into shock. I couldn't move. She looked scared and I could see that she had been crying. She looked all around the street, scanning the faces all around them for something or someone. I could tell from her scared look that she had fully expected to see me there. As I was watching her looking around, and knowing all along that she was looking for me, she turned up the street and I suddenly noticed that she was on someone's arm. I moved the scope slightly to my right and was further shocked when I saw Jean staring right at me. He looked right into my scope with a smile on his face and then turned up the street with Kate and walked quickly up to his waiting car. I sat there for a moment, watching as the car sped away with Jean and Kate both in it. I was so stunned that I couldn't move a muscle. Then, after what seemed like hours, my training took over and I started to move as I realized that Jean's people knew exactly where I was. I calmly hurried through my escape routine and quickly left New Orleans behind me."

George spoke up with a question. "Was Kate with them the whole time? What happened?"

"I didn't know at first. I had no idea what had gone wrong or who I could trust. Someone had given information to Jean about my plan. I dismissed Kate quickly because she never even knew my plan. When I caught up with her a few weeks later back in Jacksonville, I was able to confirm that, as well as the fact that she never wanted to see me again. I couldn't blame her. I had nearly gotten her killed."

"Okay," George started back again. "That doesn't explain why you're a wanted killer though. Why are the police after you if you didn't kill anyone?"

"I didn't kill anyone, then." Alex said.

George looked at his son's face and realized that his story wasn't over.

"I had scared Jean quite badly and he quickly moved to get out of the city and on his way back to Haiti. In my research and preparation in New Orleans I had found out that he had come into the country on his boat and had docked it in Bayou La Batre. I was angry and although I knew that I should not act on my anger, I beat him there. I still had not talked to Kate at this time and I was very confused because I didn't know if she was involved with Jean somehow. I kept thinking about the fact that the only people who knew what I was doing in New Orleans were the members of my Team back in Jacksonville. I did not check back with them as I made my way out across the Gulf coast and into the little town of Bayou La Batre. I just went there on my own and I patiently waited for Jean to show up at his boat. Just as I had figured, my wait was not very long. The two black

Escalades pulled up to the dock where his boat was tied up and his people started loading everything on board. I was very relived at first, when I did not see Kate with them. I did have some fear that she might be dead at the time, but I would have to deal with all of that later if I was going to do this. As Jean took his first step down onto the boat I took my shot immediately. I figured that he would go down below decks and not show his head again until they were safely out to sea. I took him down with one shot directly into his left temple. I had taken the shot from my car, which was sitting exposed across the river and I quickly put the rifle down in the passenger seat and sped away."

"I still don't understand why they are after you." George said. "You did your job. You got the man that the government wanted you to get."

"I know," Alex said. "It didn't make sense to me either."

"What happened after that?"

"Once I got to a safe place I called into the Team and spoke with Shelton directly. He told me that I needed to come back to our base in Jacksonville. I told him that I did not feel safe there and that I suspected that someone on the Team must have leaked the information to Jean about my plans. Shelton assured me that I would be safe and he told me that he would personally see to it that I would be okay.

After a few minutes of listening to him explain how he would protect me, I agreed and told him that I would come in. I waited a few days for things to settle down before I secured all of my equipment in a storage unit in Mobile and then planned my route back to the base. It was on the morning that I was packing my things to head back to Jacksonville that I first heard my name on the news. 'Alex Jameson wanted in the killing of a Haitian diplomat.' I couldn't believe what I was hearing, I started to panic with the uncertainty of not knowing who I could trust. It was then that it came to me, as I thought about who I could really rely on. It was then that I knew that the one person that would and could help me, was Michael Scott."

"You know that I would have helped you, Alex.", George retorted.

"I know that, dad. Michael was the one person that could help me though."

George conceded to his son and urged him on with the story.

"I went to Michael and he let me stay with him onboard his boat in Cedar Key. After a very short stay we figured that this was a little too dangerous for me and he set me up with a friend of his down in Key West. At first things were great down in the Keys and I was able to lay low and get a job working on a shrimp boat and I dressed as a homeless bum in order to keep people from recognizing me. Then after I was there for well over a year, some friends of mine and I decided that the island was going to hell and it was up to us to push all the rich bastards out of there. I knew at the time, that I should't get involved with politics or anything that would draw attention to me at all, but I just couldn't help myself. All the Conchs were working two and three jobs just to make ends meet down there, while the rich assholes from New England and the rest of the States up there, were buying and selling property at ever increasing prices. Times were getting to be very tough on us and we needed to fight back. We were calling our little rise 'The Wino Revolution' and before I knew it there was media attention on our little plight and I needed to run and hide once again. Michael, being my one true friend in the world at the time, decided that it was time to take me to Missing Key."

"I'm sorry that I uprooted you again, son."

"That's okay, dad. The time has come now for me to get to the truth about what happened and stop the hiding."

"How will you do that?"

"I need to go back to Florida and find my old Team. Someone on that Team sold me out and I need to find out who and why."

"Are you sure you want to do that, Alex? How will you know who to trust?"

"I'll start at the bottom. It was a small team and most of us did not have the kind of power to turn the media and government on anyone."

"What are you thinking Alex?"

"I think it was Shelton." Alex responded to his father.

"Shelton? He's a senator now, Alex. It's far too dangerous to go after him." George was getting very concerned for his son as the gravity of the situation continued to worsen.

"Who ever it was, they ruined my life and I need to find out why they did it and set all of this straight. I've been running and hiding for years now and it's time for me to stop." Alex was starting to show his aggravation.

"How can I help? I have other friends that can help us. What do you need?" George was adamant about helping his son.

"I can't bring you into this, dad. You have way too much to lose and I don't know who to trust."

"I don't care about any of that. You're my son and I will help you." Once again, George was very insistent.

"Thank you. I may need some money." Alex said.

"Whatever it takes Alex. You just ask for it and I will help you."

"Thanks again, dad."

George and Alex talked for the next few hours about what would happen next. A plan started to form very quickly as Alex talked about the people that he would need to find and the places that he would need to go.

Chapter 39

Miguel sat alone, at one of the narrow picnic tables, on the deck of the Nowhere Tiki Bar. Today was his fourteenth birthday and he had spent the morning here splicing together lines, as his father had taught him, to use onboard his Uncle's boat. He had become a very good sailor over the years and he knew that he would always be on or near the sea as he grew older. He idolized these two men that had spent so much of their time tutoring him in the ways of the sea and could think of no life that would fit him better than to follow in their footsteps.

He sat there in deep thought while he worked the shorter ropes into longer more usable mooring lines. He was thinking about his parents and why they had always lived so far apart from each other. Although he had never breeched that subject with either of them, he had once asked his uncle about it but was quickly told that his father would tell him everything that he needed to know when he felt that the time was right. As Miguel sat there with his lines he let the question in his mind grow and fester until finally he just had to have an answer.

"Dad." Miguel said, without even looking over at his father who was sitting behind the bar.

Billy looked up from the book that he was reading. "Yes?" He said to his son.

"Why do you live on this island so far from mom and me?"

Billy was a little surprised by the question. He knew that the day was eventually coming when he would have to explain to his son what the family business really was. The boats and cases of liquor and all the transient friends that he had met here over the years on this little island. What could he possibly have thought about what happens here?

Taking his bookmark from the bar top he marked his pages in 'Don't Stop the Carnival' and set the book aside. Grabbing two Coronas from the ice chest and a lime from its hammock above the bar, he walked over to his son. He tossed him the lime and said, "Slice this up for us son."

Miguel was a little excited by his father's reaction to his question. This would not be the first beer that he had ever tasted. He had become a very accomplished bartender on this island and had done a few taste tests in his time. This was however, the first beer that he would purposely share with his father. Taking his freshly sharpened

diving knife from its sheath, he wiped it on a towel and sliced the lime into eight large wedges. Adding one of the wedges to each of the cervezas he handed one back to his father who in turn held up his beer to his son and as they touched the necks of the bottles in a toast, Billy looked at his son and said, "Chin Chin, Miguel."

Billy told his son about that fateful day fourteen years earlier when he had left out of Tampico on his boat, and how the storm had left him shipwrecked on this small but beautiful little island. He explained in great detail how he and his uncle Patrick, used to smuggle alcohol and cigars from Mexico and the Caribbean Islands into the United Sates in the old days. He told his son about being a wanted man in all of the countries that he used to do business in, and that was why he could not go back to any of them.

Miguel listened to his father's story and fought back a few tears as he heard about the turmoil that he had suffered through. He wanted to help him somehow. He wanted to do something for both of his parents.

"Dad," Miguel said. "How can I help? Teach me your business and let me help you and mom."

Billy looked at Miguel and just plainly said to him, "No, son. This is not what I want for you. I simply want you to live a good life that is not confused or hindered by my life. Don't end up exiled like me. That is how you can help me."

Miguel looked back at his father and thought about what it was that he was being told. He knew that his father loved him very much and only wanted him to be happy, so he knew that the only way to respond to this request was simply,

"I promise, dad. I promise to live a good life in your honor. I love you dad."

Chapter 40

Michael and Jennifer sat at one of the picnic tables that overlooked the white sand beach from the deck of the Nowhere Tiki Bar. Friends had been coming in from all over the Caribbean for the past few days now since word had gotten out about Michael's return to Missing Key. Everyone knew that any time that he returned after an extended period away, a party would be coming on soon. The last time that Jennifer had counted, there were twenty boats tied one to another in the harbor and fifty-three people enjoying some part of the island's natural hospitality. The Shark Fin was expected to be in shortly with three more locals aboard her as well as the blue marlin that they had caught during the day's fishing trip. This would be grilled as the main course for the nights festivities. Michael had already set the fire pit on the beach and collected enough wood to burn a flame ten feet tall for the whole night. The bar was stocked and all the fresh vegetables and fruit that they would need to go with the marlin were collected and ready to be carved up. Most of the visitors were currently either enjoying the beach or fishing or just fitting in a much desired mid day siesta.

Michael held Jennifer's hand on the table as she was explaining to him that she needed to return to Chicago.

"I really don't want to leave you, Michael, but I have to get back to my studio. I've been here a week now and I love it, but I have a business to run there."

Michael knew that she was right. He did not want her to leave but he understood why she must.

"Can I visit you there some time?" He asked her.

"You better." She replied very sternly, "And I will visit you here or wherever you are as often I possibly can."

Michael did not like how this was sounding. He knew that long distant relationships were very tough. He had watched his parents make one work, but he knew the troubles that they had in doing so.

"When are you planning on leaving?" He asked her.

"I was thinking about two days from now. That gives us the rest of this weekend and then I can be back to work on Tuesday."

"Okay. I hate to see you go but I'm sure that Rosa and Jose can give you a ride into Cancun and then you can catch a flight from there back to the States."

"That would be great. You do know that I don't want to go away from you, don't you?" Jennifer was looking directly into his eyes.

"I know. I'm just really going to miss you." He responded.

Michael stood from his seat, in an effort to end the conversation, and turning on the heels of his flip flops he headed over to get a couple of beers from the ice cooler behind the bar. As he did this he looked out over the bay and could see the Shark Fin coming in with her nose high on a plane.

"Looks like dinner is on its way.", he said.

Jennifer looked over her shoulder at the bow of the boat that was quickly making its way into the mouth of the channel. Knowing that dinner was now coming into the bay she stood up and headed towards the grill to help out with cooking.

"We can still have a good time here tonight." She said as she was heading off towards the beach.

" Oh, I know.", he said. "And we most definitely will." He gave Jennifer a smile as he grabbed their cervezas and followed her out to the sand.

Chapter 41

Alex was sitting in the high back leather chair in the back of the Cessna Citation X. His father had set up this private flight for him, through the charter airlines that his company used, since they knew that he would never make it through the gate checks of standard travel. They were on the taxiway of O'Hare International Airport and second in line to take off as Alex thought about what he would do once he was on the ground in Jacksonville. The flight would take less than three hours and he had already called ahead to talk to a couple of his old friends there. They would help him get the things that he knew he would need.

George had made a call to Douglas earlier and had asked him to reserve a room for Alex at the Riverdale Inn in the city's Riverside area. The first steps of the plan were now all falling into their proper places and it would only be a matter of time before he was able to confront the very demons that had haunted him for so many years.

He sat quietly as the pilot moved the plane into take off position on the runway and pushed the throttles fully forward as they began to accelerate. As the wheels of the plane left the tarmac Alex looked out at the city in the distance and thought about Michael back in Missing Key. " I hope my message has made it through to you, Michael." He said quietly to himself.

Chapter 42

The party on Missing Key was really starting to roll now. Salvador had already cleaned the marlin and other fish that the crew of the Shark Fin had caught while Raymond and Maurice were bringing the boat back to the little island. The fresh fish were now gently smoking on the heat of the grill while the transients were slowly finding their way to the bar and beach for some dancing and mingling until the feast was served. Michael was making rum drinks as fast as he could for the carefree locals while Salvador expertly monitored the flames of the grill, like the devil himself, supervising the opening of a new annex to hell.

As Michael handed out drink after drink to the happy crowd, he was also pondering the message that Raymond had relayed to him from a radio call that he had taken while out fishing in the Gulf on the Shark Fin. Alex needed him in to fly into Miami, rent a car and then wait for his call to drive up to Jacksonville. What could he possibly be up to? He thought. Alex knew that, of all the places to go to in the States, Jacksonville was by far the most dangerous for him. Michael decided that he needed to talk to Jose and Rosa now and ask them if they could take both Jennifer and him into Cancun a few days earlier than originally planned. He hoped that Jennifer would understand that he needed to help Alex in Florida and that they would need to leave for Cancun in the morning. They would have to say their goodbyes from the airport there.

Raphael and Sonia sat at the bar talking to themselves as they waited for their drinks from Michael. Michael looked over the bar at the couple as he set the drinks down on the coasters that sat directly in front of them.

"Raphael, Sonia," he said. "I know that you've stayed longer here at Missing Key than you had originally planned, but could I ask that you two stay just a little longer? I could really use a couple of bartenders to man the bar while I'm gone for a few days."

Raphael and Sonia looked at each other briefly and then turned back to face their friend.

"Bon Viaggio, Miguel. Everything will be good my friend." Raphael said.

Michael thanked the couple for their help and then set off to find Rosa and Jose.

Chapter 43

The bonfire over Missing Key's beach was soaring as the drunk visitors to the little island shuffled back and forth from their sand covered adirondack chairs to the blaring music inside the Nowhere Tiki Bar. The party was still going strong as the blanket of stars in the sky above had reached their brightest points for the night and the haze of the Milky Way spread out to the black horizon. One by one the rugged locals were slowly surrendering to the alcohol and disappearing to the berths on one of the boats or a comfortable man made bed on the beach.

Michael and Jennifer sat on the Lucy talking amongst themselves. He had told her that both of them would be getting a ride into Cancun in the morning and also about the message that Raymond had relayed onto him from Alex.

"Isn't it dangerous for Alex to be in the States like that?" Jennifer asked.

"Very much so," Michael responded. "I think that he's going after the people that set him up and try to put some kind of end to his issues."

"Do you think that he will give himself up?"

"I don't think so. We've talked a lot about his situation and he thinks that someone from his team set him up to protect themselves. I think that he's going to Jacksonville to find out who that was and possibly put them in jail."

"You need to be careful, Michael. They could put you in jail for helping him out and hiding him for all this time."

"I know, Jennifer. I also know Alex though, and he won't let that happen to me."

Chapter 44

"Miguel," Billy said while looking down on the masked head that was bobbing just above the water, "I need you to come up and dry off for a while son."

"Okay, dad. Just let me get my things together here and then I'll be up."

Miguel had been scuba diving in the East bay for close to an hour now. Billy knew that it was time for his son to take a break and breath in some oxygen for a while.

"How far down do you think you went?" Billy asked.

"Not very," Miguel replied. I was just checking out the coral on the wall."

"Watch out for the eels and sharks down there, you know they like to hide along the shelf."

"I know, dad. I'm seventeen now and we've been over that a thousand times."

"I just don't want you to get hurt, son."

"I know, dad."

Miguel took off his fins, mask and snorkel and after throwing them up onto the deck of the bar, he climbed the ladder and sat on the edge of the wood plank floor while he stripped out of his wetsuit top and let it fall to his waist. He then went through his normal process of cleaning all of his equipment with water from the fresh cistern used for drinking before putting it all aside to air dry. Once he was finished with the process he headed over to the bar where his dad sat and reached into the cooler for an ice cold Corona.

"How was the diving today?" Billy asked.

"Really good. I found some stones in the rock among the coral. They look a little dull at first but then when the sun hits them right they shine brightly with color."

"Sounds interesting. I'll have to check them out the next time I'm diving the wall."

"I brought a few up in my bag. I'll go get them"

Miguel stood up to go and get his dive bag. As he walked towards his bag he waved over to his uncle who was walking up from the beach. Patrick waved back as he shook off the grogginess that was left over from the siesta that he had earned by working the morning in and around the garden.

"Nothing like a quick nap to recharge the batteries." He said as he walked up to the bar.

"Good for the soul." Billy replied.

"Hey, Uncle Pat," Miguel said as he walked back to the bar with his dive bag in one hand and some hazy white stones in the other. He took the stones and laid them on the bar top while setting the bag at his feet.

Billy picked up one of the stones and held it up so that he could get a better look at it.

"What have ya got there?" Patrick asked.

"I found these stones embedded in the wall during my dive today," Miguel said.

"Really?" Patrick asked, "Can I see one?"

He reached past his young nephew and took one of the stones in his hand while Miguel took his beer and leaned back in the bar stool.

"What do you think?" Billy asked Patrick.

"I'm not absolutely sure," he paused for a second as he held up the rock to the light of the sun, "but I'm thinking that Miguel may have just hit a diamond mine."

Miguel nearly fell out of his stool as he tried to sit upright.

"Diamonds?" He asked.

"I think so. I'll take these few into Key Largo this next trip and have them checked out."

"Diamonds." Miguel said again in disbelief.

He lifted his dive bag from the floor and set it on the bar in front of his father and uncle. It was full of them.

Chapter 45

Alex was sitting at the bar inside the Palace Saloon in Fernandina Beach. He knew that he was taking a big chance being in the Jacksonville area and had come directly here in a cab from the airport so that he could get things moving quickly. He also knew that he had to end all of this if he was ever going to get his life back. He chose to sit at the far end of the bar where he could see the whole room either directly in front of him or through the mirror behind the bartender's head. This convenient little spot also gave him the convenience of three exits to choose from if for any reason he needed to get out quickly.

Alex recognized his old friend immediately as he walked in through the front door of the nearly empty bar. His long hair and beard gave him a very different appearance now, compared to how he had looked years before when they traveled the Caribbean Islands together hunting very bad people. He was dressed in khaki Bermuda shorts and a T-shirt that advertised some distant bar that he may have traveled to in an attempt to escape from reality through the perfect watering hole.

Flip flops and a tattered fishing hat finished his ensemble and he walked very slowly and deliberately in the direction of Alex.

"Can I get a Jameson and water?" He asked the bartender as he made his way down the length of the bar.

"Coming right up," was the response.

"It's good to see you Jesse," Alex said. "Thanks for coming."

"What are you doing here, Alex? You know that this area is way too dangerous for you. Even though you and I are no longer on the Team, it still does exist and they are still looking for you."

"I am well aware of that. They nearly had me just over a week ago. I need your help."

"If I help you, and they find out about it, then they'll be after me too. I live around here and I'm very easy to find. Do you realize what you are asking of me?"

"I know that Jesse and I'm not asking you for any physical help. I just need you to give me some honest answers to some very direct questions."

Jesse looked at Alex for a moment and then said, "I'll tell you what I can, but I ask that you please just leave me out of this."

Missing Key

"That is not a problem. I don't need to draw any more people into this than I already have. The more people involved, the more people that I have to trust, and I can't afford that"

Chapter 46

Michael sat in one of the plastic adirondack chairs under an umbrella at The Square Grouper in Jupiter Beach. Looking out over the intracoastal waterway at the Jupiter lighthouse, on the other side of the steady water, he sipped his vodka tonic and waited calmly for Alex's call. The prepaid cell phone that he had picked up on his way out of Miami sat on a table next to him with its volume turned all the way up so that he could be sure that he would not miss Alex. Actually, he had picked up several of the prepaid phones in order to misdirect anyone that might be listening in. He and Alex would start out each call with the phone number of the next phone that they would use. This would keep them constantly changing numbers and make it virtually impossible for anyone to track them.

When Michael received the message from the crew of the Shark Fin that Alex wanted him to fly into Miami, rent a car and then just hang out in southern Florida until he called, he knew that Alex had a plan that he was working on and would need whatever help that he could get. He also knew, without any doubt, that Alex would keep him as far out of harm's way as he possibly could. Sitting in the shade of the umbrella watching the fishing boats come and go past the lighthouse, he thought about what this plan might be.

As he finished off his second drink in the hot Florida noon day sun, the little phone rang to life. Michael took the phone and as he pressed the talk button he moved it to his ear and instinctively looked around to see who might be able to listen to the conversation.

"Hello," he said.

Chapter 47

"Billy," Patrick said in a near scream to his brother. "Do you realize that what these diamonds mean? They are a god send, and we can use them to subsidize the bar here and get Maria out of working back home. She can move here with you now and the two of you can travel and be together again."

Billy was silently pondering what his brother was telling him. He could leave the island with his lovely Maria at his side and travel the world again? It had been nearly eighteen years now since he had ended up stranded here on this island. He could go to Europe or South America and just mingle around with other people. He could stay in a hotel and sleep in a bed, and take a long hot shower. Tears nearly came to his eyes as he started to think of all the possibilities that his new found freedom would open up to him.

"Have you told Maria or Miguel yet?" Billy asked.

"No, I haven't." Patrick responded to his brother. "I wanted to tell you about it first and then let you tell them."

"Thank you, brother. I can hardly wait to see them and tell them. Can you bring them both with you the next time you come out?"

"Absolutely."

Billy turned slowly and walked away from his brother. Alone in his thoughts, he walked out to the beach and sat down in the sand with his feet out in front of him and his arms and chin resting on his raised knees. He stared out across the bay and quietly cried as he watched the sun set over the orange glow of the horizon. He had seen this sunset countless times over the past several years but somehow this time it seemed all new. Billy felt like he had just been pardoned for good behavior from his island jail after serving eighteen years of his life sentence.

Chapter 48

Alex hung up the prepaid cell phone and set it down in the cup holder of his rented mini van. He was very happy to talk to Michael and to know that he had made it safely into Florida. He also knew that he would never be able to repay him for this help and that he would forever be grateful to his friends undeniable loyalty.

As he drove south along A1A through the Talbot Islands he watched as several old fishermen stood with their poles reaching out as far as they could from the decaying bridge that had been left as a fishing pier for these locals. As he looked at these men who diligently tended to their poles, a line of pelicans came up over the top of them and soared high into the air to look back down and see if they could get themselves an easy meal. When they did not see any freebies coming their way, they turned their attention instead towards the bridge that Alex was driving on and flew just outside of the long cylindrical guard rail to play in the updraft that was created by the wind that passed between the concrete structure and the roiling water below. As they tired of that, they peeled off one by one as if they were military jets breaking from a bombing run, and turning they headed back to check on the fishermen once again.

Alex continued down this scenic road and admired the beach views of the Atlantic Ocean as well as the marshlands that lined the inland side of the road. As the mangroves, trees and beach views gave way to the lines of houses that sat on the edge of the St. John's River, he began to search for his next stop. Earlier he had arranged with another member of his old team to meet him on the ferry that connected this portion of A1A over into Mayport where the road could then continue its southern journey by clinging to the Eastern coastline of Florida. As Alex pulled into the ferry's parking lot he could immediately see the car, and the man that he was looking for, just a few lengths ahead of him. He would wait here patiently though, until all the cars were securely loaded onto the ferry and they were out into the middle of the St John's River before he would get out and head over to talk to him.

He had gotten the information that he was looking for from his old team mate Jesse when he had met with him earlier at the Palace Saloon. This meeting now was primarily to double check that information, to be sure that it was correct, before he made any moves towards Jacksonville.

Alex came out of his thoughts as he saw the cars ahead of him start to move steadily in formation towards the ferry. He followed in line with all the others when the attendant waved for him to pull ahead. As he parked his car on the ferry where he had been directed to, he sat waiting to pay his toll to the attendant. He watched as the driver of the Volkswagen bug ahead of him incessantly looked all around to be sure that they hadn't been followed.

Chapter 49

Jennifer woke up at 6:00 am in her queen size pillow top bed, which sat against one of the thirteen foot walls, in the bedroom of her brownstone near Chicago's north side. She hopped out of the warm comfortable bed, feeling refreshed and put on the workout clothes that she had carefully laid out for herself the night before. Dropping to the hard wood floor she did a quick set of abdominal exercises to get herself moving, and to get the blood pumping throughout her 5 foot 8 inch frame. Afterwards she went down the stairs to her spacious kitchen and drank down a quick cup of coffee before finally making it out to do her morning run along Lakeshore Boulevard. With Lake Michigan to her left she quietly made her way south along the concrete path of the Lakefront Trail and headed into Olive Park and then on past the entrance to Navy Pier. She continued along the path and back up to Lakeshore Boulevard where she crossed over the Chicago River and then back down to the waterfront by the Chicago Yacht Club. She loved to run next to the docked boats in the morning, before people started to turn up and clutter the beauty of the scenery. Turning up Monroe Street she ran past the Green at Grant Park and gave a glance to her right letting her mind imagine the lunch crowd that was sure to be there in just a few short hours. She loved Chicago and she loved to see it early in the mornings like this, before all the business people and tourists come out and take over the streets. At this time of the morning the city belonged to her.

After a five mile run through the city she returned to her home to shower and prepare for the busy day ahead of her. She was able to get ready in what seemed to be record time and then walked the five city blocks to her studio on East Walton Street. Her assistant Shelby had already opened up for the day and had set out the mail and schedule of upcoming client meetings and photo shoots to be reviewed. This had become quite a large pile in the short time that she had been gone to Florida and Missing Key and immediately she knew that she did not want to deal with any of it. Dividing her time between daydreaming about Michael and Missing Key and staring at the pile of mail that sat in a neat bundle on her desk, she started to think ahead to what she anticipated was going to be a liquid lunch. Finally, she thought to herself, a goal had now been set in place for the day. So let's see about diminishing this pile of letters before we go.

When Jennifer walked in through the doors of the Coq d' Or, she ordered a dirty martini from the bartender from halfway across the room. She had missed this little hangout more than any other part of the city while she had been away and she was going to be sure to get reacquainted fast. Sitting down on the corner barstool she thought again about Michael and Missing Key and those gorgeous sunsets. It was tough for her to be torn between these two very different worlds. She liked them both for what they were and she also knew that she wanted to be with Michael in whatever location she was in. She missed being with him and really wanted to have one of those long talks together that she really loved.

Back in Cancun, while they were preparing to board different planes, Michael had explained to her that she would not be able to reach him for a while. Even though she had been told this, she still had tried to call him a few times, only to go directly into his voice mail, just as she expected. He told her that he would call her the first chance that he could and not to worry, but she couldn't help it. She knew that he was going to Florida to help Alex and that this was going to be a dangerous situation for him. So she felt that she had no choice but to worry. Reaching into her purse she took out her cell phone and scrolled through her address book until she found the name that she was looking for. Pressing send, she held the phone to her ear and listened nervously to the ringing on the other end.

"Hello?" The man said into his phone.

"George? It's Jennifer, I need to talk to you."

"Jennifer? He replied, "You didn't get your check? I sent you payment in full. I'll get my secretary to look into it."

"No, no," Jennifer said. "I got the check. Thank you very much. It was more than I expected. That's not why I was calling."

"Oh, good," he said. "How can I help you, then?"

"I'm trying to get in touch with Michael. Do you know where he is or how I might reach him?"

"Michael?" George said guardedly. "No, I don't know where he is. I haven't heard from him in quite a while."

Jennifer stopped for a second and looked at herself talking on the phone in the mirror behind the bar. She thought to herself that George's statement was a bit odd considering they were all together just a few days ago on Missing Key.

"I just thought that maybe you had talked to Alex." Jennifer started.

"Alex?" George asked cutting Jennifer off in mid sentence. "I haven't seen Alex in years now and as far as I'm concerned I don't care if I ever do."

Jennifer knew now that George was hiding something.

"Oh," she said. "I'm sorry. Well, I do have the rest of those pictures that you wanted. Do you want to meet somewhere so that I can give them to you?"

"That would be great," George said. "What do you think about meeting at the Signature Room?"

"Sure. That would be great. How about 8 o'clock tonight?"

"I'll see you then."

Jennifer put her phone down on the bar and took a sip of her martini as she thought about the odd conversation that she had just hung up from. She knew that George knew something and she was very eager to meet up with him and find out what it might be.

Chapter 50

Nearly a full month had gone by before Patrick was able to make it back to Missing Key with Maria and Miguel. These weeks had almost been as difficult for Billy as the first weeks that he had spent alone on this island so many years before. After Patrick had carefully maneuvered his boat into the moorings along side the tiki bar, Billy took Maria's hand and helped her off of the boat as Miguel helped Patrick tie up to the dock.

"I have news," he said to her as they finished their long embrace. "When Miguel is done with Patrick, I need to meet with the two of you out on the beach."

Maria looked into her husband's eyes for some kind of sign of happiness or sadness. She saw nothing.

Billy went over to help unload the supplies from Patrick's boat and Maria eyed him with bewilderment as they got everything stowed away into either the bar or the cave. As they got down to the last few items, Patrick looked over at Billy and said to him, "You take them now. I'll finish up."

Billy looked over at Patrick and nodded with gratitude to his brother.

"Maria, Miguel, come with me." Billy waked over towards the beach. Maria and Miguel followed him and they all sat facing each other in the circle of adirondack chairs by the fire pit.

"I have some news," Billy started as he leaned forward in his chair. "Patrick took the stones that you found in the wall of the harbor, Miguel." Billy was looking directly at his son.

"Stones?" Maria asked.

"Yes," Billy said, now looking over at his wife. "Miguel found some white stones in the wall of the deep bay when he was diving there a few months ago."

"Diamonds?" Miguel asked.

"Diamonds." Billy confirmed to his son.

"What?" Maria asked. "Miguel found diamonds while diving the wall?"

"There's more down there, too," Miguel said anxiously.

"Now, now," Billy said. "We have plenty of them and the rest are safe where they are."

"Plenty?" Maria asked. "What are you saying, Billy?"

"Basically my sweet, we're rich. We have plenty of money from the diamonds that Miguel has already brought up so that you don't have to work at all any more." Billy said to Maria, "And Miguel, you can go to college wherever you desire and after that, you have the money to make a sound man of yourself."

Maria and Miguel looked at Billy in a stunned disbelief. It was hard to take in the idea that all of their money issues were now resolved and that their lives had forever changed.

"What about you?" Maria asked Billy.

"I still can't go to the states, but I can travel most of the rest of the world. We, my darling Maria. We can travel the world."

Maria smiled as she began to realize that she could be with Billy all the time now. No coming and going from her husband and no need to have a job. Miguel would be eighteen soon so he could care for himself. She and Billy could live on Missing Key and travel the world as they wished. Finally, after all of these years apart, they would have back their life together.

"When do we start? Where do we go?, she asked Billy.

Chapter 51

George was on his cell phone in the Signature Lounge at the Hancock Building talking to Douglas who was absolutely beside himself on the other end.

"Where is he?" Douglas asked, nearly shouting. "I set up this room for him to be here last night and he still hasn't shown up."

"I know, Douglas." George said calmly. "He probably got sidetracked. You know how he can be."

"Well, he needs to get here. I had to pull out some favors in order to get him this room on such short notice. Then he doesn't show up? Do you know how that makes me look? It's disrespectful George."

"I know," George replied. "He will be there. Please just keep the room open for him. I will pay for all of the nights that the room is being held without him there."

"That's not the point George, I know that you are good for it. That boy should be here." Douglas was starting to settle down some now.

"I know, Douglas, and he will be. Please have the room held and charged to me. I have to go now. My dinner date has arrived. I will talk to you tomorrow."

George set his phone down on the small table near the large window of the John Hancock building's 96th floor. Looking out over Chicago's magnificent skyline he stood up when he saw the familiar reflection in the glass and turning, he gave Jennifer a quick hug before he motioned for her to sit down.

"We will need to talk quickly." George said to her. "I'm sure that someone will be along very soon to monitor our conversation."

"Monitor our?" Jennifer started to question.

"Yes," George interrupted. "Michael is safe and Alex has a plan to set his life straight. They are both heading to Jacksonville right now to confront the man who set Alex up years ago. You can be assured that Alex will not let Michael be harmed or involved illegally, in any way. You need not worry about him."

"George, we're having a quick and secret conversation so that people won't monitor us and you say that I shouldn't worry? How can I not worry? I want to help them. I have to help Michael."

"No, you must not do that. Let them finish it.", he said.

"Or be finished by it," Jennifer retorted. "I'm heading down there. Where can I find them?"

"You can't. I don't even know where they are. Alex hasn't checked into the hotel that was booked for him. Please just stay here in Chicago and wait. It will all be over soon."

Jennifer looked at George and then out over the lights of the city.

"I can't do that, George. I can't just sit by and wait to hear from him."

Chapter 52

"Michael," Alex said to his friend over the phone. "Things are quickly falling into place here. Can you be up here tomorrow night?"

"You know I can." Michael said.

"Good, I'll call tomorrow and give you the meeting place."

Hanging up the phone Alex turned back to the ocean surf and watched the waves of the Atlantic crash onto the sands of the South Ponte Vedra shore line. Dressed as a homeless beach bum he staked out a place along the sandy dunes to call his home for the evening. Hidden far enough away from the water, if anyone happened to notice him laying in the sand they wouldn't likely disturb him or bother to call the police.

He had found out all that he needed from his old Team mates. They had affirmed his suspicions about what had happened back in New Orleans and he felt that within the next two days he might not completely clear his name, but he would definitely be able to stop the Team from chasing him going forward. This alone was worth all the effort that he was putting forth.

Missing Key

As the sun was setting over the dunes behind him, Alex watched as a couple slowly walked hand in hand along the retreating waters of the Atlantic Ocean. The sandpipers ran along in front of them and then lifted into the air on their wings just before the lovers got too close. Alex thought back to Missing Key and to Stan and Ollie as they ran along chasing after the quick footed birds in an effort to scare them into flight. He knew that neither dog would ever know what to do with one of these long billed fowl if they were ever able to catch one and they really only seemed interested in the sport of the chase. As Alex thought back to the island and all the friends that he had to leave behind, he settled in for some much needed sleep. The morning would be coming before he knew it and he would need to get up very early to get things moving.

Chapter 53

"Now Miguel," Maria said to her son as she prepared to board Patrick's boat and leave Key Largo behind forever. "You know that we can't say a thing about the money or the diamonds."

"I know, mom."

"You can stay in the house or live with your uncle as much as you wish."

"We've been over all this mom."

"I know we have. I'm just so concerned about you."

"Mom, I'll be out to visit you and dad as often as I can. You know that and I'm off to college soon so I won't even be at home that much anyway."

"I know, Miguel. Just let your mother worry about you a little, would you please?"

"Yes, Mother. If it will help."

"It will."

Maria hugged her son tightly with tears streaming down her cheeks and then pushing herself back, she quickly turned and stepped onto Patrick's boat.

It had only been a few short weeks since she and Miguel had returned from Missing Key with the knowledge of the diamonds that would support them for the rest of their lives. Maria had gone back to work and informed her boss and coworkers that she would retire and travel the world now that Miguel had grown to be a man.

She was very happy now that Billy had the foresight all those years ago to not list him on Miguel's birth certificate, and to record his name as Michael Scott. This and the congressman, that she had befriended at Alabama Jack's on the North end of Key Largo, enabled Miguel to be accepted as a midshipman at the U.S. Naval Academy that coming up fall. With all of the years of sailing knowledge bestowed on him by his uncle and father, this seemed to be the most logical way for him to continue his education. Maria was so proud of her son. She could hardly wait to see him in his uniform. After all, she could barely even get him to wear shoes on his feet while he was growing up.

Now, as she watched her only son standing on the dock waving as she sailed away from him, Maria started to cry. She cried for herself she knew. Miguel was a man now with his own life to live and she knew that he would make her proud. Still she cried for her own sorrow of losing that one person that had depended on her for the past eighteen years.

As the boat headed out into the open waters of the Gulf of Mexico, Maria now turned her thoughts towards Billy and the life that they were about to restart. They would travel to Europe first and stay in hotels in Paris and Rome. After that the sky was the limit and they would be very sure to go all the way out to that limit. As the eagerness of starting her new life overtook the sadness of her loss, she sat by herself and watched the sun as it made its way towards the horizon. Tomorrow would be a very splendid day indeed.

Chapter 54

Alex woke up very early the next morning to get his tasks started before anyone around started to stir. He didn't want anyone to see him and then be able to tell the authorities about the bum that stole a van. He walked south, about five miles, to where he had parked his rented mini van under a beach rental home that was not being used at the time. He had taken the time to figure that if anyone happened to find the van there, they were not too likely to search for him that far away. After scanning the area closely as he approached the van he quickly got in and started it up. He then backed up onto A1A and made his way north along the coast and then headed west on State Road 210, making his way into Jacksonville. He wanted to get into position near the Naval Air Station well before the sun came up and the sooner that he was in place the more likely it was that he would just be overlooked all day.

Before he had gotten onto the interstate into town Alex had stopped off at a gas station and topped off his fuel. He also went inside and bought some food, water, and filled his coffee thermos for his stake out. Having shed most of the clothes that he had used to disguise himself as a bum out on the beach for the night, he was now wearing some dirty jeans, and a T-shirt, a flannel jacket and a baseball hat. Now he just looked like a construction worker on his way to work this morning. No one even gave him a second glance as he made his way through the gas station and then back to his vehicle to drive off. Things had quickly fallen into place since he had arrived yesterday and now he was nearly at the location where he would set things into motion. Alex felt confident in his plan and he knew that the time had finally come to make all of this straight and then move on with his life. It was also time for the people who had set him up and then kept him on the run for so long, to get all that they deserved. Today was going to be that day.

Chapter 55

Jennifer was sitting at her gate in the sprawling Atlanta airport waiting on her connecting flight into Jacksonville International Airport. Even though she knew that George had probably already called Douglas and told him not to help her in any way, he was her only connection to Jacksonville and maybe he could, at the very least, find her a hotel in town.

After dialing the number she sat and listened to it ring and was surprised when Douglas answered.

"Jennifer," he asked calmly into the phone. "How can I help you?"

"I know that George has probably already talked to you but I could use a little help."

"George?" He asked, "No, I haven't heard from George in a few days. What do you need?"

Jennifer was a little confused. How could he not have talked to George. That just didn't seem to make any sense.

"I'm flying into Jacksonville," she said.   "I'm trying to find Michael."

"Michael? He's in Jacksonville? Why is he here?"

"I'm not sure but I think that he's in trouble. Can you help me?"

"When will you be here?"

"My flight arrives at ten this morning. I'm about to board here in Atlanta."

"Oh, that's great. I'll pick you up at the airport."

"No, you don't need to do that. I can get a cab into town."

"Don't be silly," he said. "I'll pick you up after you get your bags. Call me when you land."

"Thanks, Douglas. I didn't really think that you would help me."

"Of course I will, my dear. Call me when you land."

Douglas hung up his phone and then immediately went into his speed dial.

"I can't believe our luck," he said.

Chapter 56

Maria and Billy were laying in the hammock at the edge of the tiki bar near the stern of Patrick's boat.

"Where shall we go to first?" Maria asked, turning her head to look into Billy's eyes.

"Rome," he answered. "I've always wanted to go there."

"Sounds perfect," Maria answered. "When can we go?"

"I've talked to Patrick. We need someone to stay on to help out at Missing Key. There are a lot of people who depend on us here."

"I know, but we don't need the income from here anymore. We can travel anywhere."

"I know my sweet, but we still need a home and I can't go back to the states."

"I know," she responded.

"Patrick and I figured that since he doesn't have to keep his fishing charter business any more, we would take turns running the bar and traveling. He completely understood when I asked to travel first."

"It is a beautiful place to call home." Maria said.

"I definitely know that." Billy responded with a smile, "And it's so much better now that I have you here with me, to stay."

Maria tucked her head into Billy's chest and reached her arm over him to give a big hug. She was happier now than she had been in so many years. Life was finally on their side again and they would live it to its fullest.

Patrick strolled over from behind the bar. Handing Billy an ice cold Corona with a lime, he looked at the two of them in the hammock.

"You two look like newlyweds," he said and then handed Maria a rum and coke.

"We are," Billy said back to his brother.

Maria smiled at her husband's comment. She knew that the next eighteen years would more than make up for the last eighteen.

Patrick sat in a chair and looked up into the star filled sky.

"When do you head to Europe?" He asked.

"I think that we will leave next month," Billy said. "Does that give you enough time to get back to Key Largo and get what you need?"

"Absolutely. I'll leave in two days to go back and either close down or sell the charter."

"That would be great." Billy held up his beer bottle in a toast to his brother.

Chapter 57

Alex was completely drenched with sweat as he waited in the back of the rented mini van. He had stripped down to a pair of Bermuda shorts and a T-shirt but it really wasn't helping too much. He had known that it would be like this in the hot Florida sun but he also knew that he could not give away his position by starting the engine to turn on the air. With the tinted windows on the rear portion of the van and a blanket being held up as a divider from the front, any light from the windshield was blocked off and a dim little chamber was created in the back, where he could look out without anyone looking in on him.

He had backed the van into a parking spot at the Target store on Roosevelt Avenue where the employees had their cars parked. Alex hoped that this would keep down any suspicion of why it had been be parked there all day. Outside the back window was a fence that divided the stores parking lot from the runway of the Naval Air Station in Jacksonville. Alex sat in the captain's chair that he had turned around and looked through the eye piece of the Canon digital SLR that sat mounted on a tripod. Through the eye piece, Alex's vision was multiplied as he looked on through the EF 500 mm lens. He could clearly see the hangar, on the other side of the runway, where he used to prepare with his Team for all of their missions.

There hadn't been much activity all morning around the hangar but Alex knew that there were people inside. They would be planning or preparing for an operation somewhere. There was always someone on the premises doing something. It didn't matter who was inside at work though, he was there to find one person. The one person that was looking for him. The one that had set him up years ago and would be here now because Alex had made sure that one person knew that he was there. Now as he watched and waited he stared to think about the instructions that he had given Michael. He should be in the Riverside area of Jacksonville by now. Getting all the intel that Alex knew that he would need.

Chapter 58

Michael's car was parked on the edge of the Saint John's River at the end of Margaret Street. He walked along the tree covered path into Memorial Park emerging at the large bronze sculpture that was the centerpiece for the park. As he walked along he took mental notes of areas where he or others could possibly hide from sight. Half way around the park Michael walked out onto Riverside Avenue and continued north passing in front of the Riverdale Inn. He hoped that his simple disguise of a hat and sunglasses along with an old overcoat would work. He had figured that no one would be looking for him anyway. He had no idea that he was completely wrong.

Crossing over Riverside at Lomax Street he then walked up to Five Points where Park Street, Lomax Street, and Margaret Street all intersected. Turning left on Margaret heading back in the direction of his parked car he stopped at O'Brother's Pub for a quick drink. Sitting at the outside bar he ordered a Corona from the bartender and watched in the mirror above the bar as the people and cars moved along behind him. First cerveza of the day he thought as he took the prepaid cell phone from his pocket. He dialed the number that he had written down on the book of matches that he had gotten from The Square Grouper.

"Hey," was the answer from the other end.

"Alex," Michael said. "Riverside is all set. The park is only one block away and has enough people wandering around to make it safe. I can see at least six quick ways out of the park, in an emergency, as well as several areas to hide if needed."

"Great," Alex said. "I have one more thing that I need you to set up for me and then I just need you to wait for my word."

"Let me know what you need me to do," Michael responded.

Chapter 59

Patrick was on the line of sight radio with Billy as he closed in on Missing Key.

"Looking like another gorgeous day in paradise," he said to Billy.

"Best I've seen in a long, long time. My sentence ends today," Billy responded.

"I know that it does. You all packed and ready to go?"

"Oh yeah, have been for a few days."

"Great, I have a surprise for the two of you."

"Does it have anything to do with that boat following you?"

"As a matter of fact it has a lot to do with that boat following me."

Patrick realized that Billy had probably been watching him through the "big eyes" that they had mounted near the top of the north side hill on the key.

"We'll be in the harbor in just a few minutes," Patrick continued. "I'll tell you more then."

Billy turned away from the glasses and headed back down the hill to the Nowhere Tiki Bar.

Maria had been cleaning things up around the bar so that she could feel good about leaving it behind while they set out for Europe. Their bags were all packed and sitting near the end of the bar. After unloading the supplies from Patrick's boat they would get a ride from him into Porto Morales on the Yucatan Peninsula where they would spend a week before heading to the Cancun airport and then on to Europe.

As Patrick maneuvered his boat into the harbor Billy and Maria could see the bow of the Hatteras that was coming in behind him. They helped Patrick tie up to the dock and then headed over to help with the other boat. Billy read the name "Lucy" painted on the boards of the bow as he heard Maria yell in excitement.

"Miguel!"

Billy looked behind the wheel of the cockpit to see his son expertly docking this boat in the harbor. He smiled as his chest heaved with pride and a tear formed in his eye. Patrick walked up behind his brother and said, "I'd like to introduce you to your new boat brother. This is The Lucy."

Billy looked at Patrick and tried to form words. Nothing would come out of his half opened lips.

"Enjoy her brother," Patrick finally said.

Maria had climbed aboard the Lucy and up to the cockpit where she attacked her son with hugs and kisses.

"I can't believe that you're here," she said.

"I'm here to drive your taxi." He responded as Billy came up the ladder behind them. "I'm taking you to Porto Morales while Uncle Patrick holds down the bar. That is, if you'll let me drive your boat.", he looked at his father.

Billy took Miguel in his arms. "You can take my boat any time you want. You're the best captain on the seas."

"Well, let's get your things then. You two have a trip to make."

Chapter 60

As the limousine pulled up to the small door of the hangar, Alex focused in the lens and started snapping off digital pictures. The limo sat there for quite a while without any movement from it or the hangar and then the back door opened up. Alex found himself holding his breath as he could see the shoes of the passenger hit the pavement. It seemed like another minute passed before the grey hair of Senator Shelton appeared on the other side of the long sleek car.

"Finally," Alex said. "I knew you would be here."

Alex continued taking pictures and then was very surprised to see a very familiar face get out of the limousine. He hadn't seen Kate since everything had happened all those years ago. Why was she with Shelton now? He struggled to make sense of her being there as he took pictures and watched as they disappeared into the hangar. He continued to watch and continued to go over those days, that they had been together. Did she work for Shelton back then? Nothing seemed to make any sense. As Alex continued to watch, the large overhead door of the hangar started to open and the Team's jet was pulled out.

Kate and Shelton spoke for a few moments and then she boarded the plane as the Senator got back into the limo. After watching the plane taxi out to the runway and then take off, the limo pulled away from the hangar and headed back for the main gate.

What was all that? Alex wondered. I have to find out what Kate was doing here with him. It just doesn't seem to make sense. Alex packed up his gear and moved back to the front seat of his rented van. Time to get showered and try to put all of this together.

Chapter 61

Michael had made the final arrangements that Alex had asked him to make. It was getting to be late afternoon and now he, too, was in place. Alex would be arriving at the Riverdale Inn soon and everything would start happening, very quickly, after that. He sat anxiously in his position waiting for Alex to call him with his instructions on moving.

Alex parked in the Inn parking lot, off of Lancaster Street. Instead of walking in through the back doors, he walked along the sidewalk to the front door to be sure that he was seen. After checking in with the front desk, he headed up to his room and quickly jumped into a hot shower. There was no reason to spend much time actually moving into the room, he wouldn't be there very long.

After the short but refreshing shower he put on some fresh clothes and headed back downstairs to the bar. When he entered he saw that Shelton was already sitting at the table near the window. Alex looked to the bartender and ordered a vodka tonic and walked over to the table where Shelton sat all alone.

"Nice to see you again sir," Alex said to him.

"Why don't you have a seat?" Shelton said back. "I've been looking for you for a long time now Alex and then you show up back here? In my own back yard? Why are you here?"

"I want this to end. I want my name cleared and my life back."

"What life? You were a hired killer. You can't go back to that. The team has moved on."

"I know that, but there still seems to be some familiar faces there."

The Senator looked at Alex, as the bartender brought the drink. Alex paid him immediately and then looked back at Shelton, as the bartender walked away.

"What familiar faces are you talking about, Alex?"

"How long has Kate been working for you?" Alex asked.

Senator Shelton was taken aback for a second. What did Alex think that he knew and more importantly what did he actually know?

"Finish up your drink, Alex. We'll take a walk. The walls have ears."

Alex took a small sip of his vodka tonic. He knew that his last line had put the Senator on the defensive and he wanted to keep him there.

"I have some questions for you, Sir."

"I know that you do Alex, and you will have even more of them shortly. You had better drink up."

Alex finished up his drink and the two men headed down the front stairs of the Inn to the sidewalk on Riverside Avenue. Turning left they walked the block to Memorial Park where Alex could feel the eyes on them. Shelton had not brought the police, Alex knew that he wouldn't do that. There were people here though, watching and waiting for the signal to pounce.

The two men walked the oval shaped sidewalk around the perimeter of the park. Slowly, they passed couples exercising and others walking their dogs. Both of them eyed each person that they saw to see if there were signs that they had maybe a little too much interest in them.

Alex spoke up first asking again, "How long has Kate been working for you Sir?"

The Senator was silent for a moment before answering.

"Kate doesn't work for me, Alex," he said.

"I saw you two together. I know that the team flew her somewhere earlier today."

Shelton smiled. "Doing a little reconnaissance? You were always the best, Alex."

"What is her connection? Why was she with you?" Alex barked.

"Alex, Kate does not work for me. She works for the drug cartel in Haiti. She was working for Jean when you killed him," the senator said. "She was keeping an eye on you. It was her job to protect him from you."

"That can't be true. How did she know who I was?" Alex was confused now.

Senator Shelton was silent once again. He thought hard about how to answer Alex. He finally settled on telling him the truth. Alex wouldn't be leaving this area without an escort from some of the team members. There was no reason for him to worry about any retaliation.

"Alex," he said. "Kate was working for Jean and Jean was working for me."

Alex stopped and looked at the Senator. He was surprised by this response. His investigation over the past few days had already led him to this conclusion and he was wondering how he would get Shelton to admit to it. Now he just throws it out there? What was he up to?

"You, Sir?" Alex responded. "What do you mean?"

"I mean that I am the head of the Haitian cartel, Alex. I was using Jean as a figurehead who could do my footwork and I was using you to get rid of the competition."

Alex was surprised again. He didn't realize the extent of the Senator's involvement. He was also very angry at the fact that he had been used by him.

"You were using me to sell drugs? I can't believe that you were doing that."

"Believe it, Alex." Shelton said.

"Then I'm going to the police with this."

"No, you're not."

"You don't have enough team members to stop me Shelton, and once I tell them what I know I'll be pardoned and you'll be in jail."

"I don't need the Team, Alex."

Senator Shelton looked to the park opening where a limousine was sitting with its blackened windows all closed tight. He motioned to the car with his hand and the back door opened. Alex watched as Douglas stepped out of the car followed by a woman. As Douglas moved to his left, he could see that the woman with him was Jennifer.

"What the hell is this?" Alex could feel his pulse increase.

"Insurance," Shelton replied. "You will come with me and in trade I won't harm her."

"You bastard. She doesn't have anything to do with this."

"And this has nothing to do with her. So leave her out of it Alex and come with me."

Alex looked over at Jennifer. Douglas was holding her close to him and walking in their direction. Jennifer had a steady look in her eyes. It wasn't fear or any tears. It was just pure anger. Alex could see that she was very upset and about ready to explode. As they got closer, she looked right at Alex and said in a furious tone.

"Where is Michael? Is he okay?"

"Michael? He isn't here," he lied.

From behind Alex and Shelton a figure moved past quickly and approached Douglas head on. Stopping just short of running into him the man stopped to the surprise of everyone.

"George?" Douglas nearly screamed, "What are you doing here?"

"What am I doing here? Douglas, what are you doing here? You used me. You were my friend. You used me to track down my son. How could you betray me like that?"

"Dad!" Alex shouted. "You shouldn't be here."

"I am here Alex and this son of a bitch is not going to get away with this."

Senator Shelton realized that the situation was quickly getting out of control.

"Alex," he said. "You need to get your father out of here right now."

Douglas never saw George's fist before it hit him in his left temple. The blackness was sudden and he wouldn't even remember it until several hours after he had come back from his state of unconsciousness.

George grabbed Jennifer's arm and started running in Alex's direction. Alex pushed Shelton back away from him and yelled out to his dad to follow him. As they jumped over the short pillared rail the trio landed in the Saint John's River. By the time Shelton made it to the rail Michael had already arrived in the small Boston Whaler and was preparing to fish them all out of the water.

Senator Shelton couldn't believe what was happening. Douglas lay flat on his back on the sidewalk and Alex was about to get away with the knowledge of his involvement with the Haitian drug cartel. His heart sank and his anger rose as he watched his three escapees crawl into the boat and speed off along the shoreline of the river. He could feel his career coming to its end.

Chapter 62

On their third day in Porto Morales, Billy and Maria sat in the plastic chairs on the terra cotta tiles of the Ojo de Agua. Waiting on their dinner of fresh red snapper, they enjoyed a ceviche and guacamole appetizer as they looked out over the quiet beach to the waters where they had just returned from snorkeling. Eduardo and Marcelles had taken them out to the reef in their open fiberglass dive boat and the four of them went on an adventure that included eagle rays, lobster and the red snapper that they were now waiting on.

As they sat in the shade of the thatched roof that rose up over their heads, they talked about their future travels around the Caribbean and Central and South Americas. Billy was thrilled to be away from Missing Key for the first time in nearly twenty years. He felt as if a tremendous weight had been lifted from his chest as he breathed in his new life and future as a man who had finally been freed from his self imposed prison.

The loud crack of the first shot echoed through the open patio and into the restaurant and bar. The few patrons that were inside, quickly turned to see what had happened. Once they saw the gun in the man's hands they threw themselves to the floor for protection. Billy's first reaction was to stand up in disbelief as he saw his wife's left cheek explode and turn itself inside out as the blood flew from her mouth and covered their food just before her lifeless head hit the table. He didn't even hear the second shot as he felt the searing pain building in his lower abdomen. Still on his feet, he backed to the knee wall that separated the patio from the beach. He turned his head to the left as he heard his name being called out to him from a familiar voice.

"Señor Billy." The voice said to him.

Billy looked at the face of the man behind the revolver that was pointing directly at him.

"Señor Billy. You should have stayed dead, after all these years. You should have stayed dead so that you would not have to die now."

"Juan." Billy gasped. He was fully aware now of the bullet that had lodged in his stomach. He was starting to feel lightheaded and sat back on the wall. "Why?"

"Do you remember the day that you left from Tampico into the storm? Do you remember that day? Where have you been?"

"I remember that day vividly, Juan.   That day changed my life forever."

"It changed my life too, Señor."

"What happened Juan?"

"The federalies did show up that day.   They arrived out on the dock just as you were reaching the breakwater. They had no intentions of going out into that storm to get you and risk their own lives. They settled for me."

"You?"

"Yes, they took me off to prison for ten years." Juan's hand was shaking.

"I'm sorry, I didn't know."

"Now you do know, Señor. While I was in prison, my wife took my young son and moved away from me. She did not leave me anything that could help me to find out where she had gone. She left while I sat wasting away in prison for you, and I have not seen her or my son since. I lost everything that day."

"Juan, my god, I swear I didn't know."

"I lost everything because of you Señor.   Now you will lose everything too."

Billy looked at Maria's lifeless body slumped over the table. He began to cry as he stared at her.

"Why did you have to kill her? She did nothing to you."

"Because you had to lose everything too. Before you died."

Juan squeezed the trigger of the revolver that he still had pointed at Billy. The bullet entered Billy's skull just above his right eyebrow. He never felt the pain as he flipped backwards into a heap on the beach below.

Chapter 63

"Jennifer, what are you doing here?" Michael yelled over the roar of the outboard engine.

"I was looking for you. I found out that you were here with Alex and I was worried about you."

Michael liked the fact that Jennifer cared enough about him to worry. He did not like her being involved in all of this though. He looked over to Alex.

"Did you get what you needed?" He asked.

"I got him to say enough to have the police look into his actions. As long as the video turns out, that is."

"I placed the camera on the statue in the park like you asked. I can go back later tonight and get it," Michael said.

Michael moved the Boston Whaler near the wall at the small park at the end of Elizabeth Street. Alex jumped out of the boat and onto the shore.

"It's the white Nissan at the end of the street," Michael yelled to him, "The keys are on the rear tire."

George jumped over to the shore as well.

"Where are you going, dad?" Alex asked.

"I'm with you, Alex," George replied.

"No, dad. I need to hide again for a while until we get that video and have Shelton in custody. He's going to do whatever he can now to catch me. I have too much on him now."

"That's why I'm with you. You need my help. You're my son, Alex. You have to understand that I have to help you."

"Let's go, dad." Alex said, knowing that he did not have the time to argue about this now.

The two men ran off towards the street as Michael turned the small boat back out into the river and sped off with Jennifer.

Michael and Jennifer moved along the tops of the shimmering river water, only slowing when they hit the no wake zone of the Ortega River. Steering the boat into a slip at the marina at Ortega Landing, Michael quickly tied the boat up and turned to take Jennifer's hand, to help her from the boat.

"Come with me, Jennifer. I have a car in the parking lot here." He said. "We need to go and hide for a few hours."

After the two reached the rental car that Michael had picked up in Miami, he started the engine and drove off. He headed in the direction of the safe place that he had picked out to hide in until they could safely move once again. Jennifer sat quietly at first and then decided that she had questions that she needed answered.

"Michael," she said. "What's going on here?"

"Alex is trying to clear his name."

"Okay, but what does Senator Shelton have to do with all this and why did Douglas take me hostage?"

"Alex believed that Senator Shelton had something to do with him being set up all those years ago. He wasn't sure how but he just knew that there was some connection. We set out to see if we could get him to confess to whatever he was doing."

"I still don't understand. Why did Douglas take me hostage?"

"Douglas is working for Shelton. He grabbed you as leverage so that Alex would just go with him quietly."

"I thought that Douglas and George were friends. Who does that to a friend?"

"Exactly what we thought. Douglas was just getting close to George so that if he was ever around Alex, he would be there with him.

"That's terrible," Jennifer said.

"Yes, it is and now he will pay the price for his choices."

"Pay the price? What does that mean?"

"Nothing specific. We all make choices in this world and we all have to answer to them eventually." Michael said.

"When do we go after this video?" Jennifer asked as she thought about Michael's comments.

"In a few hours," he said. "I hid the camera in plain sight but you would have to be looking for it to find it. Alex had a remote with him to start the recording and I had told him where to stand when talking to Shelton. It all went pretty good except that we didn't foresee him grabbing you. It was lucky for us that George showed up when he did."

"I'll say it was. He saved my life."

"And Alex's as well," Michael added.

Michael pulled into a parking spot near the stop light on Margaret Street.

"This is where we're hiding?" Jennifer asked, looking up at the Starbuck's sign in front of her.

"Hide in plain sight," Michael said. "They never look there, plus it's a very public place so that if they do find us they'll have trouble getting to us."

"But we're not even a block from Memorial Park," she said.

"I know," Michael responded. "Crazy isn't it."

Jennifer just looked at Michael before they both got out of the car and headed in for lattes.

Michael knew that it seemed odd to be hiding here but he also knew that he wasn't hiding. He was here on purpose. The Senator and Douglas were now the ones on the defense. They wouldn't be looking for Michael. They wanted to get Alex, but right now they were scrambling to cover up all the loose ends that they could in case this blew up. Michael was here now to watch the park and make sure that no one got that camera before he did. He would wait and watch until he felt that he could safely get the camera down from its perch high above in the wings of the bronze angel that was the corner piece of the park. Patience was the name of the game now.

Chapter 64

"What do we do now, Alex?" George calmly asked his son.

The pair had driven off in the rented Nissan that Michael had left for them. They went directly to where Alex had parked the mini van that he had been using earlier. Swapping vehicles they now sat in the back of the van in the Target parking lot looking once again out over the runways of Naval Air Station Jacksonville towards the hangar that was used by Alex's former team.

"Now we wait." Alex told his father. "We wait for Michael's call telling us that he has the video camera and we watch that hangar and record any movement that we see around it. Shelton is likely to come here eventually. He will either be trying to get away himself or possibly trying to get rid of something. We'll be here to record it." Michael pointed at the camera mounted on the tripod.

"I can't believe that Douglas was using me like that. I could have killed him when I saw him there holding Jennifer like that. I really wanted to kill him."

"I know, dad. Don't worry about Douglas. He will get what's coming to him. We just need to be sure to get Shelton. He was the one in charge. He is the one we want. His fate will be different. He has to go down in a very public way. People need to know what he is doing. Otherwise, he'll be a martyr and I can't have that."

George looked at Alex and could only nod in agreement. He knew what his son was saying was true. He could only hope that whatever Alex was going to do next would be the right move.

Chapter 65

Douglas was very agitated as he sat in the leather reading chair of his apartment's office. The left half of his face was stinging with pain as his cheek started to swell from the right hook that George had planted there.

"How could I have let him get to me like that? I was so surprised to see him there that I just couldn't move."

"That is no longer any concern, Douglas. We have to start thinking about damage control. We need to step up our search for Alex and now we will need to kill him once we find him because he knows way too much. Lucky for us that he jumped into the river though, if he was recording anything that I told him in the park then the water will have destroyed that. It would then come down to a wanted killer's word against that of a U.S. Senator. I think that I can handle those odds."

Shelton walked over to the window of Douglas's little office and looked down onto Riverside Avenue. As he raised his gaze up to the statue at the other end of Memorial Park he could see a couple strolling hand in hand near the waterfront where Alex had escaped into the river a few hours earlier. As he watched, the couple separated and the woman took a camera from around her neck and started to take pictures. The man went over to the statue and began to climb onto it's base and pose while the woman clicked away. Why must people deface property like that? he thought to himself as he turned from the window and walked back into the room to where Douglas was still sitting.

"I need to get back to Washington," he said. "You stay here and rest up while I go back and start to do a little damage control before anything is made public. I will need to get a new story started with the press and get the local police involved so that Alex will not get away from me again."

Chapter 66

Alex had just hung up his cell phone from the second of two calls that he had been on. The first call came in to him and was very brief and to the point. As soon as he had finished that call, he immediately went to his speed dial and made an outgoing call. Now, with both calls over, he watched through his camera lens as the limousine that he had spotted earlier came rolling back in front of the familiar hangar. He watched silently and clicked off picture after picture as the Senator boarded the small jet aircraft that had been parked in front with its crew preparing for a quick departure.

As Alex continued to watch, the small jet taxied out to the end of the runway and then quickly picking up speed first the nose wheel lifted and then the rest of the plane followed along and it was airborne.

"Looks like were all set, dad," Alex said. "The Senator is in for a little surprise."

Chapter 67

Michael was sitting at the bar in Alabama Jack's enjoying some Conch Fritters when one of the Card Sound locals walked in through the wooden gate that served as a front door and navigated his way through the maze of tables to the bar.

"Michael.", he said as he brought over a copy of the Key West Citizen. "I have some very bad news."

Michael took the newspaper and read the bold letters that his friend was pointing to. It was a story that started in the lower left corner of the front page and read ***Long lost local man shot dead in Mexico***. He quietly read the story about his mother and father being shot and killed in a Mexican hotel and bar by an ex-convict. The story said that the local police had arrived just after the killer had shot the couple and jumped down to the beach. He started to run off in the direction of Cancun, but they quickly caught up to him. The man then turned towards them, with his gun still in hand, and they were forced to shoot him dead in the surf of the Caribbean Sea. His name and reasons for the shooting were not given in the story.

Michael set the newspaper down on the bar. Turning in his stool he got down and walked over to the railing that overlooked the mangrove swamp leading to Biscayne Bay. He cried the only tears that he would ever shed for his parents right there, as he thought about the tragedy of their life. After a few long moments he returned to the bar and held up his Corona to his friends seated at and working behind the bar.

"To Billy and Maria," he said, "any couple should wish to have the tragic life and love that they had."

The bar was silent as everyone held up their drink in a toast, to the man and woman from this little island community that never let the ocean, or hurricanes, or life, stand in the way of their love.

Chapter 68

"Lieutenant Garcia." Senator Shelton shouted into the intercom. "Lieutenant Garcia, why are we landing? Pilot, I know that we're not anywhere near Washington yet. Why are we landing? What's going on?" Senator Shelton was getting more upset with the silence that was being returned to him. Looking out the window Shelton recognized the sprawling flat city below them. Was Garcia out of his mind? They hadn't even been flying in the right direction.

"Lieutenant Garcia!", he yelled into the silent intercom. "Why are we in Miami?"

Garcia broke the silence. "Senator," he said. Alex Jameson called me just before you arrived at NAS. He played me the audio of you admitting to being a Drug Cartel leader. The D.E.A. is waiting for you on the runway here in Miami." The intercom was silenced once again.

Shelton looked out his window at the blue lights flashing on the runway below. He could feel his anger inside. He could feel his contempt for Alex. He tried in vain to assure himself that this could not possibly be happening.

Chapter 69

The article in the Florida Times Union was headlined simply, **'Local businessman dies in own bed.'** The story was buried towards the bottom of page five in the local section between a story about a woman whose flower beds had received national attention and an ad for a restaurant in the Avondale district. The article said simply:

Local businessman and real estate investor, Douglas Wilson died last night in his bed. Although Mr. Wilson had some bruising to the left side of his face, the authorities said that they did not appear to be related to the cardiac arrest that had happened somewhere around one o'clock a.m. The medical examiner stated that Mr. Wilson appeared to have taken a fall that may have caused the contusions to the face and that after he had completed the autopsy it was concluded that there were no signs of any foul play. "It looked as though he had just lived a full life," he said.

The front page headlines of the Florida Times Union on that same day read **'Florida Senator Julian Shelton arraigned on drug trafficking charges**.' This story was a bit longer.

Chapter 70

Michael and Jennifer were sitting in the adirondack chairs watching the sun set over the key's west bay.

"I love this sunset," Jennifer said. "I don't believe that I could ever get tired of it."

"I know," Michael responded to her. "Greatest secret in the world."

"I couldn't agree more," Alex said from the chair to Jennifer's right. "Who wants another cerveza?"

ABOUT THE AUTHOR

Scott was born in Bay City, Michigan in 1968. He and his family spent time traveling during his younger years and that fostered an insatiable urge in him to see as much of the world as he could.

Sailing the Great Lakes as a boy, Scott loved to go into the ports of Northern Michigan and Canadian cities and wander around the streets to take in the sites. Having relatives in the southern United States, he and his family would spend many of their springs in Alabama, Georgia and Florida visiting and touring the attractions of these wonderful states. As he grew older he would spend time with his friends traveling Michigan on bicycles and then by car as they started to travel to ski resorts in the state during the winter months. After graduation from high school, Scott joined the Navy and was able to get his first taste of foreign country travel. There was no looking back for him.

Today Scott lives in Jacksonville, Florida which he has found to be a great location for starting out on his travels in most any direction. If not flying to his destination, you can find him loaded up on his BMW motorcycle and heading off in whatever direction he feels that he can find a new adventure.

11339316R00162

Made in the USA
Charleston, SC
16 February 2012